ECOMASTERS
A Planet in Peril

Book One:
The Pathfinder

By
Donna L Goodman

Illustrated by
Luisa Faletti

Ecomasters: A Planet in Peril by Donna L Goodman
Book One: The Pathfinder
Published by Isabella Media Inc
270 Bellevue Ave #1002,
Newport RI 02840
www.IsabellaMedia.com

© 2020 Isabella Media Inc

ISBN-13: 978-1-7357256-1-1

For permissions contact: requests@isabellamedia.com

This book is dedicated to the memory of my mom
Sue Etta Yaffe Goodman, who taught me
about creativity, love, laughter and commitment
and in honor of my amazing dad
Robert Sherman Goodman, who has 'been in my corner'
every day my life.

My children, Stacey, Lindsey and Elliot have inspired Coral's journey, and
mine. And my granddaughter Emma, who is co-author of another book
with me and her new sister Sophia

With most sincere thanks to a team of amazing professionals:
Katherine Grasso
Brenda Windberg
Free Expressions Literary Service
Madeline Drabkowski
Monica Kramer

Cover Art by Peter Bragino

Contents

Chapter One

I open my eyes, a huge smile already stretching my cheeks tight. I've been waiting for this day for, well, days. Leaping out of bed, I open my blinds, loving the way their pink slats make my room look rosy, and peer out at the sky. Another hazy, hot, humid day. How many does that make in a row now? I've totally lost count. I stare up into the foggy sky, trying to remember what the sun looks like, until I feel a huge weight, a Peeve-sized weight, against my leg.

"Morning, boy," I say to the gigantic, blackish-bluish bear of a dog at my feet. "Are you excited for today?"

He cocks his head like I'm not making sense. "We're going to Jasper's house, remember? And then to his community garden."

Peeve barks, which I take as a sign of his excitement. "I know, right?! We'll be planting flowers and, hopefully, getting lots of vegetables for the soup kitchen." Saying it out loud makes my insides warm. After seeing more and more people struggling lately, it sure feels good to do something, anything, to help.

Almost like my thoughts make it happen, I hear the sound of blaring sirens, the wails bouncing wildly off the high-rise buildings in my neighborhood. It seems like I've been hearing more ambulances than usual lately. The sidewalks have been more like a hot stove for weeks, and, seriously, I can't even count the number of times I've seen someone faint. The ambulance drivers don't need to wait for a 911 call. They just go out and pick people up... the lucky ones, that is.

Just knock it the heck off, I want to scream. Living in New York City is complicated enough. We sure don't need temperatures working against us too.

Even though the extreme heat upsets me, I know I'm beyond lucky. I live in a nice building with a swimming pool and all the air conditioning I can handle. Sure, things aren't always so great inside our apartment, but you can't have everything. And today, I remind myself, I don't have to deal with any of it.

Pushing past Peeve's giant body, I grab a quick shower, find some good gardening clothes, gather my wet hair into a ponytail, and brush my teeth. Then, practicing my best smile, I head for Dad's study. It's early, way before most people would be up and working on a Saturday but, if I know my Dad, he's already been at his desk for hours. And today, that doesn't bother me at all. Today, I get to escape these walls and do something important.

"Hey, Dad," I say to his back, eyes transfixed on the flowing water captured within the glass wall behind him. If I waited for him to turn and look at me, I'd be waiting forever.

"Hi, Coral," he murmurs. "You're up early."

I nod, though he can't see me. A strange symbol on his computer screen catches my eye—like a cross between a volcano and a waterfall—and I step a little closer before I catch myself. He doesn't like me looking at his business things. "Yep. I'm just going to grab some breakfast and then head out."

He stops typing and looks my way, every bristle of his scrub-brush haircut standing at attention. "Head out where?"

My heart flutters, but then I remember he forgets things a lot, at least things having to do with me. "Jasper's house, remember? I asked you last week, and you said it was okay."

He scowls. "I don't remember saying that."

My sigh feels like it starts in my toes. What a surprise. "Can you just say okay now and then? We need to get to his community garden before it gets too hot outside. I'll be home way before dinner."

His dark eyes narrow, and he glances back at his computer. A little shiver runs through me as he closes the document and the symbol disappears. I try to hold the picture in my mind, clinging to the way it makes me hopeful and curious, but it fades away when his annoyed expression swings toward me again. "Where is this garden?"

"In Jasper's neighborhood. East Harlem."

My Dad nods. "That's right. He's the scholarship kid." I shrug. "Yeah, he's really smart. So, can I go?"

He takes a deep breath but says nothing. The tick of his favorite clock, a giant metal gear full of smaller, overlapping gears, echoes inside my body. Finally, he pushes away from his giant wooden desk, then stands and extends his hands out in front of him, thumbs up top and fingers as straight as the maroon pinstripes in his shirt. "You know I just want to keep you safe, right?"

I don't know what to say. Since when is my life unsafe? "I guess so."

"And you know your friend lives in a questionable neighborhood, don't you?"

I sigh and cross my arms. "His house is very nice, Dad. And you've met his parents. They're nice, too."

He shakes his head, short bursts of movement that make it seem like I'm the unreasonable one. "This isn't about his parents or his house, Coral. Things are changing in the city, and in the world for that matter. Life is getting more dangerous by the day. We have to be careful."

A strangle tingle climbs up my back, almost like my body wants me to be worried, but I refuse to go there. "I grew up in this city, Dad. I know how to be careful."

"You can't prepare for what you've never encountered, Coral. I'll let you go to Jasper's, but I'm calling one of my security guys to go with you."

My mouth goes goldfish on me, falling into a big O. "Are you serious?"

"Completely."

"But that'll make me look like such a freak! I might as well write 'rich kid' on my forehead and hope the people at the garden don't laugh me off to the sidewalk."

Something changes in his face, creases I never noticed before, and all I can do is stare. He blinks a few times, and then smiles, but only with his mouth. "I know this isn't what you want, and I'm not trying to scare you. I just have to keep you out of harm's way."

Man, what a crock. "Out of harm's way? I'm not asking to go skydiving or anything. What's dangerous about community gardening?"

"I can't explain everything right now. You're going to have to trust me."

I shake my head, not even trying to hide how annoyed I am. It shouldn't be hard to trust my Dad, right? And it didn't used to be. But lately, I kind of feel like I'm living in some sort of science experiment, like I'm a lab rat instead of a kid. "I have a right to know what's going on, especially if it means I need a bodyguard and have to give up my friends."

My Dad's hands fly high in the air. "Oh, for crying out loud, Coral. Stop being so dramatic. No one said you can't have friends." He points toward the hallway. "Go to your room. Think about what really matters and let me know when you figure it out."

My whole-body warms, full of a white-hot pressure I've never felt before. "This is stupid," I tell him. I turn and walk to the door, suddenly super relieved to get out of this room and away from its secrets.

"You'll thank me someday."

"I don't see that happening," I say and put an extra stomp in my step. This is definitely not over. If he won't tell me what's going on, I'll get the answers for myself.

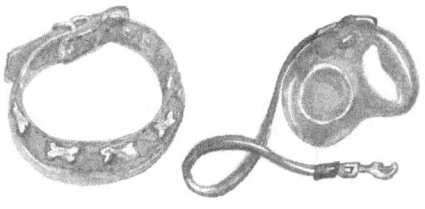

Chapter Two

I slam the door to my bedroom, so my Dad doesn't come looking, and go right to my laptop, flipping its bright pink cover up with a snap. He's not the only one with computer skills. Another siren screams outside my window, and I think back to the panicky wave I heard when I woke up. The tingle starts up again, this time at the back of my neck. Did something happen in the city? Is that why he's being so weird?

I peer outside as I wait for my computer to start up, searching the streets and rooftops for scary things. One roof over, a group of people stares down at the street, one guy even using binoculars, almost like they're expecting a parade, but everything else looks mostly the same. Hot, sure, with that thick, shimmery air that means it's going to be sweaty, but it's summer. That's what happens in summer.

A thud on my door startles me, and my heart keeps pounding for a moment, thinking my Dad decided he has more to say. But when an annoyed bark accompanies the second thump, I chuckle and hurry to open it. Poor Peeve. I promised him a day outside; he's probably been sitting next to the drawer where we keep his leash this whole time.

"Hey, buddy. I'm sorry. Change of plans, I guess." I scruff his ears and scratch his head.

He leans into the scratch, then pulls back and looks at me like I've forgotten something. "What?" I say.

Peeve barks.

"I hear you. I'm disappointed too."

I pat his head one last time, then sit in front of my computer and try to remember everything my Dad said. I search for 'changes in the world' and find all kinds of links about massive climate change, virus, fires, war and politics, social media and cybersecurity. Since we started our 'new normal after the coronavirus' none of this stuff has been a hot topic for my Dad. I try 'problems in NYC,' and then 'recent problems in NYC'. Headline after headline pops up about the heatwave, and then, water. Water Shortage! Water Crises! The price of produce and the city's aging water delivery and sewer system. More on climate change causing the heatwave, and again, water. Since I was a kid, it's true – the world has changed. Our world has changed, here in in New York City. All because of this heatwave making the water crisis even worse. I pause. *Why* is none of this stuff important to my Dad?

I flop back in my desk chair, frustrated. Everything has shifted since I was a kid – that's true. But why does he think I need a bodyguard to go to Jasper's house? For crying out loud, I've been walking Peeve on my own since I was eleven. And a water crises doesn't make a city unsafe…or does it? It just doesn't make sense for him to start worrying now.

My brain flashes me a glimpse of that symbol on his computer, and I squeeze my eyes shut, trying to remember all the details. I know I saw a volcano, but the rest is fuzzy. A teardrop? Is someone sad about a volcano? Or maybe it was a waterfall, like the glass wall behind his desk. Could it be a resort? Is he planning a vacation?

When I search for 'waterfall volcano,' I find mostly pictures of lava pouring into the ocean, and when I try 'crying volcano,' I just find articles and videos about the creepy screaming noises volcanoes make when they're erupting. An irritated groan slips out, and Peeve lifts his head to study me.

"It's okay, boy. Just not finding what I need."

He snorts and lowers his chin to his crossed paws, which makes me smile. Even when I'm stuck in my room, or when my Dad's too busy for me, I always have my friend. Peeve will never leave my side, that I know for sure.

As I look at him, a small flame ignites. My Dad said to think about what really matters, and I realize that one doesn't need much thought. This whole day was supposed to be about what matters. I reach for my phone.

"Hey, Jasper."

"Hey! Where are you? We're leaving for the garden soon." His voice squeaks a little on the last word. It's been doing that a lot lately.

I sigh. "There's a complication."

"Your Dad?"

"Who else!" I flop down on my bed, frustrated but grateful that Jasper pays attention, and I don't have to explain. "He's being extra weird, though."

"Weird how?"

"Honestly, kind of paranoid. He made it sound like it's dangerous in your neighborhood and said he has to protect me."

There's a long silence on the other end. "Seriously?" Jasper says. "Has he ever even been to my neighborhood?"

A hot wave of shame passes over me. I know it doesn't really belong to me, but it still burns. "I'm sorry. He's clueless about a lot of things."

"Yeah, well. Not your fault."

I sit up, full of a new plan. "You know what? We had important plans today, and it's not right for him to stop them. Give me some time to slip out of here and then I'll be over."

"Sneaking out seems like a really bad idea, especially if he's all worked up about something," Jasper says, the squeak returning.

"But it's not fair," I murmur. "He's being ridiculous." "I just don't want you to get in trouble."

"He probably won't even notice I'm gone."

"But what if he does?"

I reach for Peeve's head, and the soft, floppiness of his ears makes me feel better. "You're right," I say in a long huff.

"We'll try again another day," Jasper tells me, though I can tell he's not so sure.

"Yes, we will. I'm not going to live my whole life in this bedroom because my Dad's gotten really paranoid."

"Let's hope that's all it is." I hear a sound in the background, then a muffled response from Jasper. "I have to go, Coral. My mom's ready to leave. You okay?"

I chew my lip and try to suck it up. "Yeah, definitely. You guys have a great time. Tell your mom I wish I could be there."

"Okay. I hope your Dad chills out."

"Yeah, me too," I tell him, then snuffle back the tears until I'm sure he's gone. It's dumb to be crying, I know, but suddenly my brain is full of pictures—Jasper and his mom, laughing and getting their hands dirty as they plant and gather vegetables; my Dad walking me around the apartment when I was still small enough to stand on his feet; my mom giggling at the two of us and then sweeping in to join the dance.

Before I know it, I'm sobbing over Peeve's comforting ears. He whimpers a little and licks my face, and it helps, but the empty place inside me just keeps stinging. Usually, I can tell myself something that makes it okay for my mom to have left us, even if part of me always knows it's just an excuse. Today, though, I have nothing.

Nothing but a wish, tiny and tender as a flower bud, for my mom to sweep in and gather me up one more time. I want to remember what she smells like, want to see my own hands in the shape of hers, want to see that smile that made me the center of the universe. Mostly, I just want to belong to someone, or even some*thing*. I want to be pulled close instead of sent away. And I want to change whatever I have to change to get me there.

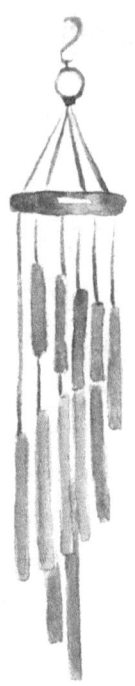

Chapter Three

I don't know how much time passes, but when the highly patient Peeve snorts in my ear, I realize I probably dozed off with my arms around his neck. I sit up and rub my tear-crusted eyes as Peeve gives me the 'can we go out NOW?' look. Poor guy. He probably needed a walk a long time ago.

"He can't make you stay inside, can he, boy?" I say with a kiss to his head. "Maybe I should just let you pee in the living room to make the point."

Peeve lowers his head and whines, clearly correcting me.

I grin. "I know. You're right. It's just so tempting, you know?"

He stares at me, and I can tell he's not tempted in the least. "Okay, buddy. Let's get that walk."

Once I say the magic word—the one I think he likes even better than *eat*—my giant friend leaps into motion. He lunges for the door with a bark, and I shush him as I grab his collar and open it. "Hush, boy. Let's not make this more dramatic than it has to be."

Peeve chuffs in response, and we make our way back to my Dad's office, even though it's the last place I want to be. Mostly, I hope that, by now, there's no one else in there with him. He's been working at home for a couple of weeks, and all sorts of people keep showing up to see him, people I've never met before. Which is saying a lot, since I've spent a pretty good amount of time at his office over the years.

When we reach the doorway, I exhale hard. It's just him, thank goodness. I notice his eyes are still glued to the computer screen, and that same symbol sits in the upper left corner of the document. My curiosity sparks, but I push it back. I can't tackle everything at once.

"Peeve needs to go out, Dad."

He clicks the document closed but doesn't look at me. "Don't be gone long."

I try to hide my sigh. "He needs some exercise, or he's going to be pain to deal with later."

My Dad turns to me. "Fine. Walk him around. But stay close by."

"Okay." I wish my eyes were lasers, that they could scan his face and identify what's so different about him. A little burst light up my mind, as much feeling as memory, an echo of my pounding heart and late-night shouting that disappears into mist before I can grab hold. I bite my lip and shake it off—won't do any good to get upset now—then back myself out into the hallway and hurry to the leash drawer. Can't let my Dad change his mind.

Peeve stops his happy dance long enough to let me hook leash to collar and then he drags me to the door. When I open it, he rushes into

the hallway, his tongue lolling and his face full of puppy-joy. I step out behind him and, when I turn to close the door, see something unexpected at my feet. A small box, wrapped in brown, parchment-like paper, sits just outside the threshold.

I pick it up, surprised at its weight, and flip it over to look for a shipping label. There's none, but a small note is tucked into one of the seams. I pull it out, then gasp. It reads: *For Coral.*

That's it. No other clues. I turn the package back over and shake it a little. The rattle tells me there's something metal inside. I start to open it just as Peeve decides he's had enough. He barks and lunges down the hall, almost taking my arm off. Poor guy. This just isn't his day.

"Hold on, boy," I tell him.

His eyes say he most certainly will not hold on. I purse my lips, thinking. Time for countermeasures. "Want a treat?"

The ears go up and the feet stop. He studies me, and I flash him a big smile. "Give me a second. I'll even grab you an extra one."

He takes a few steps my way and, taking that as agreement, I stuff the box in my pocket and lead him back into the apartment, grateful I hadn't closed the door yet. Holding my finger across my lips, a sign I know Peeve understands, I run into the kitchen, grab two treats, and hurry him back out the door. In the hallway, I scratch behind his ears and give him one of his rewards. Then I guide him into the elevator, out the front door, and into the little courtyard on the side of the building where I know Mr. Dobbins, our Doorman, can't see me.

After I get my big, furry guy to sit, I plop down on a bench and give him the second treat. As he happily chomps, I pull the mystery box out of my pocket. Feeling a little stunned, like I somehow forgot my own birthday, I carefully peel away the parchment paper—in case I want to search it for clues later—and lift the lid.

A note with my name on it lays on top, and as weird and fluttery as it makes me feel to be known, there's no way I'm reading it before I see what's inside. Moving the note aside, I find the oldest, oddest compass I've ever seen; at least I think it's a compass. There's a needle in the center, and four possible directions with hashmarks in between. Instead of N, S, E, and W, though, there are four symbols I don't recognize. Honestly, they don't even look like letters. What in the world?

I sit there, feeling a little deflated. Sure, a compass is cool, but I'm not even sure that's what it is, and I definitely don't know how to use it. I don't really know what I wanted the surprise to be, but it suddenly feels like this wasn't it. I set the box beside me and drop my chin into my hands with a huff.

In the final stages of treat enjoyment, Peeve lifts his head and studies me, eyes concerned. "It's okay, boy," I tell him, remembering the note. I give his ear a quick scratch and then open it.

Change awaits, in every direction.

A shiver dances across my shoulders and, for a second, I feel the weight of unfamiliar eyes. I look all around me, but see no one, and the shiver passes. I tell myself I'm being silly. I'm a random kid in a private courtyard. There are no eyes.

Below the cryptic message, I see an address. I don't recognize the street, but a wave of gratitude washes over me that it's in New York City. Whipping out my phone, I type the address into my GPS, pretty much ready to search this minute. But then I see how far it is—like twenty minutes one way—and all of my nerve clumps in my throat. This will take some planning.

Stowing the compass and the note in my pocket, I grab Peeve's leash. "Gotta pee, boy?" I say.

The happy relief in his face makes me want to hug him. What did I ever do to deserve such a sweet, patient friend? Wheels turning, I walk him around the block, trying to come up with a reason for Peeve and me to go out again later. Disappointing old compass or not, I know this address is going to burn a serious hole in my pocket until I figure it out.

He stops at his favorite fire hydrant, a bright yellow one on the street behind ours that has somehow looked freshly painted for my entire life. As I wait for him to finish making his mark, a city bus flies by, the bright turquoise banner, looking like a long splash of water, spanning its whole side catching my eye. A series of clocks seem to look back at me, each one smaller than the last until time literally disappears at the back of the bus. A gasp flies past my lips, and I think my heart skips a couple of beats.

What am I thinking? If not now, when? Isn't that what the bus is telling me? My Dad's already in a 'no' mood. There will be no yesses later on.

"C'mon, boy," I say to Peeve, tugging my phone out of my pocket and pulling up the address a second time. "Let's go find out what this is all about."

Chapter Four

As we step up our pace and cross the street, the hot city air rises up from the pavement and slaps me. A smell drifts my way, just a hint of something I've never smelled before, like sweat and baking dirt and scorched flowers. It makes me sad, and a little nervous. It feels like I haven't been out in the world for a very long time, even though it was only yesterday. Things are just changing too fast.

Peeve doesn't seem to notice, and he drags me along like usual. His jaunty steps bring my smile back, and I follow him happily, watching the blue black-streaked fur at the top of his head glint in the sunlight. Weighing in at more than a hundred pounds, he is not always the easiest dog to walk with, and he's definitely not taking it easy on me today. When we get to the end of the second block, he pulls me to the left, toward his next favorite 'tinkle target,' a light pole plastered with multi-colored flyers at the entrance of our neighborhood park.

"Not today, boy," I grunt as I tug his giant body the way we need to go. Fighting his momentum almost knocks me on my butt, but he lets up at the last second, so all I do is wobble. "We'll go to that park soon, I promise. I know you have dog friends to catch up with."

Peeve snorts, clearly a little miffed, but quickly takes the lead again. He pulls me along for a while, then stops and decides on a shady spot to make his jumbo-size poop. I smack my head, realizing I've forgotten to bring a bag to pick it up. I make a mental note to come back to this spot again later to clean it up and push ahead. Right now, I have a mission.

Blocks later, as the skyscrapers shrink, I realize I don't know this part of the city as well. I check my phone to make sure I'm going the right way. Six more blocks and a right turn, then three blocks and a left. My nerves wake up as I calculate, making my steps a little less steady. I sure hope my Dad's wrong about all that danger. And I sure hope this trip turns out to be worth the risk.

Wrapping Peeve's leash around my hand a couple more times, mostly because it makes me feel better to have him a little closer, I glance around us and try to get my bearings. I see 110th street, which suddenly sounds familiar. Didn't Jasper say the community garden is on that street? For a second, I get all rebellious, thinking I might as well just do all the things I'm not supposed to do in one day. But then my spirits dip as I realize I have no idea how far down I'd have to go on 110th or what I'd be walking through. I guess it's not really smart to push my luck.

Peeve slows down, looking more than a bit ragged from the heat. My heart flutters a little, reminding me that I'm already way out of my comfort zone, and that I really don't know what I'm walking into. This probably wasn't my best-ever idea, following strange clues around New York City. But how could I resist? And the box had my name on it. MY name. No kid—or adult, even—would be able to ignore something like that.

The weight of the compass against my leg reassures me. I have to do this. Ten more blocks max. We can make it!

Peeve sniffs a centipede on the sidewalk, and I pull him along before the creepy thing slides right up his nose. That's a complication I do NOT need. Plus, my protector has to be on his guard. My Dad's voice slips back into my head, and I realize I sound like him, all nervous and paranoid. Whatever this is, I decide, it has to be a good thing. I mean, it's all so mysterious and interesting. How could it be bad?

Before I know it, I've made the first turn. Three more blocks before the next. I slow Peeve down a little, wanting to look around a little bit before we get there.

"Pretty nice around here, isn't it, boy?" I say, patting his flank.

He gives a soft bark of approval and tries to veer off into a little courtyard in front of a brownstone. I pull him back, but I don't blame him. It's pretty here, like a real neighborhood full of real people, names belonging to familiar faces instead of labels on mailboxes. It's still a lot of cement, sure, but here and there, trees and shrubs grow right out of the ground instead of from fancy planters. No doormen. No elevators. Every door just a few feet from the street instead of stacked high in the sky.

I take a slow, deep breath. It feels different, like the air feeds my lungs instead of just passing through. Peeve nearly yanks the leash out of my hand, and I pull him back before he bounds after a squirrel. I guess this place feels pretty good to him too.

"C'mon, boy. We have to keep moving."

He snorts his annoyance but keeps walking. I reach down to scratch his back and, when I straighten, crash right into what feels like a pillar but turns out to be a person.

"Watch it!" The girl, probably older than me but not much, backs up with a snarl and eyes me like I just tried to pick her pocket. Her dark gray eyes startle me; they're almost like metal, like robot eyes.

"I'm so sorry," I stammer, hoping my voice is louder than my beating heart.

"You and that dog are going to hurt someone."

"He's really well-behaved, I swear. I'm sorry."

She crosses skinny arms over her chest. It hits me that she's wearing a hoodie. In this heat. Weird.

"You live around here?" Her eyes dart around, reminding me of a hawk, which makes me the field mouse.

"Not far."

"It's probably not safe for you to be walking around alone."

I work hard to keep the shock from showing on my face. What's with all this danger stuff? Is there something in the water? "I do have this giant dog to protect me," I say and flash a grin, hoping to lighten her up a little.

She cocks an eyebrow. "You still need to be careful. We all do." With that, she glances over one shoulder, then the other. "Get on home now," she says, giving me a scowl that makes her look a little like a gargoyle.

I gasp and step away. This girl's a little bit terrifying. Luckily, she just shakes her head and starts walking like she's late for dinner.

Stunned, and a little weirded out, I watch her go. She glances back twice, frowning and shooing me away. What is her problem?

"C'mon, Peeve," I say. "We're almost there." We walk to the end of the block and, before we make the turn, I look behind me, hoping the girl has disappeared. Instead, she stands in the middle of the next block, watching me. A jolt rocks my body and, at the last minute, I turn right instead of left.

I walk past a few houses, then duck behind a stairway, planning to lay low for a few minutes. Peeve has other ideas, and they don't include hiding from weirdos on the street. While he sniffs and tugs and licks my face, I peek over the stairs, making bucketfuls of wishes that I'll never see that girl again.

After way too many heart-thumping minutes, I stand and lead Peeve back the right way. As we walk, it seems like the compass gets warmer in my pocket. You're just rattled, I tell myself, and keep walking.

There's no sign of the girl by now, and I finally exhale. I reach into my pocket for the mysterious note, wanting to check the address, and I swear I feel the compass move. It's like it jumps in my pocket.

"Breathe, Coral. You're just spooked." I give my cheek a little pat as Peeve nudges my thigh with his head. "Thanks, boy. I'm okay," I tell him and pull out the note.

I stare at the number, 234, then glance up at the house in front of me. Two-thirty-four. Huh. What are the odds?

"We're here, Peeve," I say and take a good look at the brownstone.

My breath catches. I've never seen so many crystals and prisms in my life. They're everywhere, hanging in windchimes, poking up from the flower beds and flower pots, decorating the handrail leading up the stairs. Even the doorknob looks like the top of a fairy queen's scepter. Something in me warms as I look at it, and I feel certain I've seen it, maybe even touched it, before.

Peeve sets to sniffing, taking an inventory of every flower and leaf in his path. For a second, he pulls me away from the brownstone and, as I tug him back my way, it again feels like something moves in my pocket.

Trying to shake off the strangeness, I walk up the stairs and face the door. The doorknob prisms dance in the sunshine, like raindrops set free to celebrate the billions of colors of the rainbow. My heart pounds as I knock, the beats echoing each other, making this moment feel bigger and bigger. My fist stops, but my heart keeps going, filling my head and my ears, heating the bottoms of my feet. The rhythm inside grows stronger and faster while I wait, and I worry I'll explode before I find out if anyone's home.

Peeve dances next to me, chuffing his impatience.

"Hang in there, boy. We can't leave yet." I tell him, disappointment seeping in like a bank of thunderclouds as the waiting moments pile up.

I lift my fist one more time, hoping like crazy that the adventure isn't going to end this way. This can't all come down to a useless walk across the city, especially since I'm probably going to be in so much trouble by the time, I get home. I pull all of my breath into my chest and knock as hard as I can, hard enough to make Peeve look up at me, ears pricked forward.

I sigh and gather up his leash. "C'mon, boy. I guess it's not going to happen." I turn his big body around, then watch his ears prick up again at a sound behind us.

Glancing back, I see a small, smiling woman, whose toffee colored skin glows like a dew drop, standing in the doorway. "You're finally here," she says and steps back to open the door. She presses a hand to her heart. "Please come in, Coral. It's so lovely to see you."

When she says my name, my body goes hot and cold at the same time. It's not exactly a surprise, but it sounds strange—but also familiar—coming from her. I turn back and look at her, then step forward because...I mean, who wouldn't?

Next to me, Peeve hesitates. I put out my hand to soothe him just as the woman bends down and looks him in the eye. "You'll both be just fine with me, sweet Peeve. This I promise you."

With a satisfied sniff, Peeve trots ahead and pulls me through the door. I follow along, trying not to be shocked. It takes *a lot* to move my giant dog but, if he's okay, I am too. Now to find out what this all means and why I'm sitting right in the middle of it.

Chapter Five

The door closes behind us, but I barely hear it. It's all I can do to keep my mouth from hanging open. We're in a house, but it feels like we're still outside, maybe even more like the outside than when we stood on the sidewalk.

Plants are everywhere—huge, prehistoric-looking plants, fruit trees in giant pots, rows and rows of herbs and flowers and ferns on shelves and tables in every direction. Just like when we were walking through the neighborhood, it feels easier to breathe here. The air itself seems alive.

The woman leads us out of the foyer. We step into a big room with a long blue sofa and a worn leather chair in the very center, with tables and tables of plants lining the walls around them. "I'm Miriam," she tells me and holds out her hand. "You and I haven't seen each other in a very long time."

My eyebrows arch so high they sting a little. "We've met before?"

"Oh, many times. You were very small, though, so I'm not surprised you don't remember me."

Wow. I did not expect that answer. Amazement stretches my mind wide. How could I forget someone like her?

I start to ask more, then notice Peeve across the room, about to tug an apple off a small tree. I sometimes share my apple slices with him, and he loves them, so it makes sense he'd try to serve himself. I don't want him to eat the seeds, though, so I hurry to stop him. Plus, it's rude to snatch other people's fruit off their trees. At least I think so. It hasn't really come up before.

"Whoa, boy," I say and tug the apple from his mouth. I notice a small clipboard in the apple tree's pot, leaning against the trunk. I glance around the room and spot these clipboards everywhere, in every planter and on every table. Is this woman a gardener or a scientist? I turn to face her. "Why am I here?"

Miriam smiles, her eyes as green and shining as the greenery around her. "You're here because it's time."

"Time for what?"

"That remains to be seen."

I purse my lips and try to be patient. I guess she's not much for straight answers. Maybe I need to back things up a little bit. "How do we know each other?"

Her smile widens, and she sits on the sofa and pats the cushion next to her. "Come, Coral. Let me explain."

Finally. I walk Peeve her way and make him sit before I take a seat. Then I wait.

Miriam reaches over and lays her hand over mine. It's warm at the center but the fingertips are cool, and her touch makes me remember, and then forget, a faded something. Color fills my mind, almost like

someone tipped a can of lavender paint over my head. I look into her eyes, hoping to understand.

"I have known of you since before you were born, and I met you on the very day you entered the world."

All I can do is blink and hope this will make sense soon.

"Your mother and I knew each other very well. I was her research assistant and her very good friend." She squeezes my hand and then clasps hers in her lap. "If my name does not sound familiar, it's because you knew me as Mimi."

Mimi. Mimi. I say it to myself over and over, and each time, something new flashes in my mind. Ginger cookies. Peppermint tea. A nubby blue sweater. A small metal ball, like a dozen rubber bands cast in copper, shining at me from the top of a very messy desk.

I look up at her again and see her this time, like my mind turns the camera lens and brings her into focus. "Mimi. I remember a Mimi," I murmur, the crinkle lines around her eyes and the deep dimple—just one—dotting her cheek tumbling me into a warm bubble of deja vu.

Her face relaxes. "I am so happy to hear that."

"But why am I here *now*?"

Miriam takes a deep breath. "Clearly, you've come because you're ready."

I want to flop back in my seat. I usually like puzzles, but they're driving me a little nuts right now. "Okay...what am I ready for?"

"That, too, remains to be seen."

"No offense, Miriam, but you don't sound like a scientist."

That makes her laugh, and the sound jolts me into a memory. I see her, and my mother, nodding and talking as they work, then bursting into laughter as I stumble toward them in my mother's lab coat. Tears flood the rims of my eyes, and I clap my hand over my mouth.

"You now remember me as a scientist, don't you?"

I nod.

She nods too. "Very good."

"Where's my mom?" The question, the one I never allow myself anymore, pops out before I know what's happening.

She reaches out for my hand again. "I know you miss her. And I know she misses you."

My heart does a funny jumping thing. She knows my mom misses me, present tense? "So, you're in touch with her? You know where she is?"

"In theory."

I can't take it anymore. I pull my hand away and, this time, lean away from her and against the back of the sofa. The compass shifts in my pocket, and I pull it out. "Why did this show up at my house?"

Miriam winks at me, her bright eyes seeming more pixie than human. "Now we're getting to the right questions."

I try to think of an answer for that one, but I'm stumped.

"It appeared because you asked."

My brain itches a little. "I asked for a compass?"

She raises a pointer finger in the air. "You asked for change." I give a little nod. That part is true.

"In your case, this will be no ordinary change, no typical right turn instead of left. You, my dear Coral, have a destiny, and by making the request you made today, you have set that destiny in motion."

My pulse starts a warning beat. Friend of my mother's or not, this is sounding a little crazy. I lean forward, desperate to understand every word.

"Much of what comes next will not make the kind of sense you're used to. It will not make the kind of sense you've been taught should rule the world. But that word—should—is key. Should belong to man, not nature, and they usually cause more harm than good."

I gulp, suddenly feeling like I'm in school, though I have no idea what class. A weird urge to run home rushes through me, like a tidal wave is coming and I might not survive out here on my own. I gulp again, desperate for more air. Maybe I don't really need to understand any of this at all.

"I can tell you're overwhelmed, so let me just say this. You have a mission, Coral. While I know its intention, I am not allowed to give you specifics. I can tell you that, by accepting the compass, you have activated your unique destiny to be Pathfinder of the ECOMASTERS. As Pathfinder, you will find a path that leads —in ways I cannot explain— to three other girls of your age, and together, you will become the drops which lead to a wave of change."

All I can do is stare at her. She looks normal, and kind, not like someone I would usually fear. I glance over at Peeve, who's curled up and dozing near her feet. He doesn't seem bothered by her at all.

"I don't know what to say," I tell her finally.

"Understandable." She smiles. "And irrelevant. The process is set in motion."

Now I stand. It feels like I've been here for days. "Well, okay then. I guess I'll be going."

She jumps to her feet and pulls me into a hug. "It has been beyond wonderful to see you again, dear Coral. We shall have more time together in the future but, for now, let the compass be your guide."

"Sure," I tell her. "I'll go wherever it takes me." As I say this, I wonder if she's ever really looked at the thing. Even if I promise to follow it, I have no idea how to read those symbols, or if it even has all the right parts inside. Don't compasses use magnets?

"Excellent. Excellent. You will be an exceptional Pathfinder."

"You bet," I tell her, so ready to get to the door. "C'mon, Peeve. Let's get home."

He looks up at me, clearly happier to keep napping, but I gesture for him to get up and he finally pushes his big legs to a stand. I grab hold of his leash and, following Miriam, tug him out of the room. Just before I get to the foyer, I glance down at one of the plant tables. A copper ball lies there, nestled between some ferns, exactly like the one I pictured earlier.

My mouth goes dry, and I think about doing something I never do: stealing. I mean, would she really even miss it? And why do I care so much? I start to walk away—because I'm not a thief—but then this strange, bubbly energy rolls through my body. I freeze, a little scared and a lot curious. What the bleep is happening to me?

Faster than I knew I could move, I reach out, snatch it, and tuck it into my pocket, then tug at my t-shirt so it flops loosely around my middle. Whatever this is, whatever it used to mean, I know in my bones it's also part of my mom. I may have walked across New York City to end up with more questions than answers, but at least I can leave with a little piece of her.

"Take the greatest of care, Coral," Miriam says as she opens the door.

"You too," I tell her.

She rubs my shoulder as I pass, then reaches down to pat Peeve's hind end. "Keep the watch, Peeve. We're counting on you."

He gives a sharp wag of his tail, almost like a soldier's salute, and keeps walking. I follow him to the street, mystified but more determined than ever to figure out why everyone's so worried about my safety.

Chapter Six

I sneak back into the apartment like a jewel thief, making sure I don't jiggle the key in the lock or close the door too hard. I even hold Peeve by his collar as we walk, keeping his tags pressed to my palm so they don't make any noise. Even with all of this, I totally expect to get caught, and punished, since the clock shows I've been gone for over three hours, and no one watches the clock like my Dad.

I get to my bedroom free and clear, though. At least it seems like it. There's not even a note on my bed or desk instructing me to come to his office when I get home. He does that sometimes, when he wants to make sure I know I've broken the rules. But there's nothing, which is either super scary or crazy lucky.

Just to be on the safe side, I climb into bed and try to make it look like I've been home napping for a while. If he already knows, it doesn't really matter, anyway. Peeve jumps up and snuggles next to me, and his big, warm body makes me feel calm and safe. Turning my back to the door, I pull the compass and copper ball out of my pockets and take another look.

Rolling the ball around on my bed, I try again to remember why I feel so sure it's connected to my mom. My cheeks flush a little, because it's the one and only thing I've ever stolen. Even if it doesn't mean anything specific, it makes me feel closer to her, like it's a little key to who she was back then, and maybe even who she might be now. Wherever she is.

Let the compass be your guide.

I picture Miriam's face when she said that, how happy and certain she looked. Why does it matter so much? And why me?

Glancing down at the compass, I realize for the first time that it looks like it's made of the same copper metal as the ball. Is that a coincidence? I flip it over, checking for marks, inscriptions, buttons, secret compartments, but there's nothing. I peer at its face, trying to figure out the marks could mean, but they just look like random squiggles. How in the world can this thing lead me anywhere?

And then it hits me: I need to know more about my mom. My body stings at that thought, since no kid should ever have to think such a thing. Moms are supposed to there, checking homework and putting notes in lunch boxes, smiling over birthday cakes and hanging family pictures all over the house. They're not supposed to be gone—like VANISHED— with no reason or explanation, just a stupid little excuse like 'the world needs her expertise.' What about me? What about what I need?

Frustrated and restless, and working really hard not to let the tears take over, I move out from under the covers, which makes Peeve grumble. "You can keep napping, boy. I'll be back in a bit." I rub his head between the ears until he sighs and closes his eyes, then set out to see what else I can learn about my mom.

Putting myself in ninja mode, I slip out of my room, making sure to close the door so that Peeve can't follow. I definitely don't need his 'bull in the china shop' style of help. Then I tiptoe down the hall and across the living room toward my Dad's office.

Once I hit the hallway, I know I'm home free. He's snoring, nice and loud, which means that, if he wakes up, the silence will tell me. I peek past the doorway and see him sprawled on the couch. Best of all, his phone is nowhere near him, so maybe he didn't set an alarm this time. Good thing he was up so early this morning!

Knowing every minute counts, I dash back through the apartment to my Dad's bedroom. I pause in the doorway and listen to make sure I can still hear the snoring. There it is, loud as ever.

I step inside and realize I'm holding my breath. I've been avoiding this room for a very long time. The furniture's the same—though it looks a lot smaller than it used to—but the comforter and curtains are totally different, all autumn browns and golds. I close my eyes for a second, picturing the airy greens and whites that used to make my parents' room feel like a leafy fairyland. I guess I understand why that might have been hard for my Dad to look at once our fairy took flight. My stomach starts to hurt a little, and I open my eyes and go back to the doorway for a snoring check. All good.

My first stop is the closet, but there's not much in there. My Dad's not exactly a flashy dresser, and it doesn't look like he holds onto much either. There are two shoe boxes on the shelf, but they just have shoes inside, so no mystery there. I try the dresser next, looking through his sock and underwear drawers, his cargo shorts drawer, and his belt and handkerchief drawers. Nothing.

I start to think this is a bad idea, not worth the risk. And then it hits me. Where do I stow things, I want to keep but I don't want anyone else to notice? Under my bed, of course.

Heart pounding, because I probably shouldn't be in here much longer, I drop to the floor. And there, pushed all the way up to the wall, directly under the headboard, I see a box. It's not big, but it's not small, and I scurry to the other side of the bed to reach it.

My hopes rise and fall as I pull it toward me. What are the odds that this is actually what I'm looking for? I hold my breath and drag it out into the open, then gasp when I see 'Sophia' in sharp black letters on the top. Holy cow, I think, as press my hand against the cardboard and that odd, bubbling sensation takes over my body again. I seriously can't believe I found something, or, honestly, that my Dad left something here to be found.

The bad news is that the box has flaps, not a lid, and the worse news is that the flaps are taped. Chewing my lip, I try to decide if I risk cutting it open. Maybe it would be smart to make sure I have more of the same kind of tape before I do this.

"What in the world—"

I freeze. Crumbs. I should have taken a snoring reading before I went after the box. I drop my chin to my chest, take a deep breath, then push myself to my feet and face him. His eyes, as dark and narrow as I've ever seen them, make me shiver.

38

"Hi," I murmur.

"That's what you're going with? Hi?" His sneer makes him ugly, more like a movie villain than my Dad.

I swallow hard, fighting for whatever words will do. "I...um...I was just thinking about Mom today, and I started to wonder if any of her stuff was still here. I went to ask you, but you were sleeping."

"So, you just skipped the permission step entirely."

A tiny flicker of fury warms my chest. "Well, she is my mother."

He raises just one brow. "Meaning what?"

I lick my lips. It's so hot in this room. Did the air conditioning go out? The eyebrow demands an answer, and I try to stand taller. "Just that I have a right to know about her."

"You do know about her. All you need." He bends down and picks up the box.

That sets me off. I suddenly don't care if I get in trouble—which I certainly will—or if I hurt his feelings—which I probably already have. He knows things about my mother, my *missing* mother, that he's never shared. Who does he think he is?

"She wasn't just yours," I tell him, my voice wobbly.

"She was never mine," he says, much quieter than I would have expected. I start to feel a little bad, but I also see an opening. "Then give it to me." He scowls, looking more confused than angry. "What?"

"Give the box to me if you don't want it. I need to know more about her."

His eyes drill into mine and, for a second, I think I see a tear at the corner of one. Regret washes over me, and I take a step closer. Maybe he just needs a hug.

"Don't even think about it," he snaps and lifts the box out of my reach. "Nothing in here will make you feel better about her abandoning us."

I feel my mouth pop open and the air leave my body. He might as well have kicked me in the stomach. I watch him, blinking and swallowing back tears I will not let him see.

"Go to your room," he says. "And this time, you will not leave, except to use the bathroom or get something to eat, without my express permission."

I can't find a single thing to say. Is whatever's in that box worth this? As I stomp out of the room, I make a vow to find out. No matter what.

"I would call them friendship trees"

Chapter Seven

Days later, I'm still ticked off. Not to mention bored out of my mind. By now, it feels like I've re-read every single book I own and texted my friends until I just couldn't stand feeling so left out and alone. He hasn't even been letting me walk Peeve, instead having his assistant come to the house twice a day, which just makes life feel all wrong.

One thing's for sure, though, this fight is not over. Maybe I shouldn't have sneaked into my Dad's room, but he shouldn't have kept things from me. And he definitely shouldn't have been such a jerk when he caught me. While I sit on my bed and hug Peeve, sniffing his musky, grassy fur, I decide, once and for all, that my punishment shouldn't have happened either. It's just not right.

The restlessness comes back, making my head buzz and my legs tingle. I need to get out of this apartment. I have things to think about, things Miriam told me it's time to figure out. If I stay here, I'm just going to be sad and ticked off. If I stay here, there will be no change.

Of course, at this point, getting out will be pretty close to impossible. I have no idea how to do it. Peeve lifts his head, yawns, and nudges my hand like I might have something in it. I think about a treat for him, then realize I haven't eaten anything since the muffin I wolfed down for breakfast.

"C'mon, boy. We're still allowed in the kitchen, so let's go get a snack."

Eyes and ears newly alert, he dances to the door and waits for me. My heart lifts a little, just knowing I can always count on him. His tail wags, telling me I've got that right, and we slip out of our pink-painted prison cell and into the hallway.

We're almost to the kitchen when I hear a knock on the front door. I stop and reach out to grab Peeve's collar and show him the silencing finger, then listen hard as I tiptoe forward. The last thing I want is to have to make nice in front of whoever might be at that door. I'm not ready to be the well-behaved daughter just yet.

I hear my Dad open the door, and I hurry to peek around the corner, keeping my body out of sight. A well-dressed woman, one more person I've never seen before, fidgets in the doorway. Her dark-colored suit seems to be sopping with sweat, and she faces my Dad with a very serious expression. "I need a word with you in private," she urges.

He says nothing, just nods and guides the woman into his office, closing the door firmly behind them. I glance down at Peeve, stunned. Not what I planned, but hallelujah; this is definitely our chance.

Just like that, I'm ready to fight back. I grab some treats, some string cheese, an apple, and my water bottle, clip my keys to the belt loop of my shorts, make sure the compass is back in my pocket, then slip us out the door and into the elevator.

As we ride down, I think about the woman at the door. She looked really upset. And my Dad let her in without even a question. What is *that* about? I don't remember any of the visitors looking like that before.

We hit the lobby without anyone else getting into the elevator, which makes me breathe a little easier, and then we don't see anyone on the way out the door either. The less witnesses the better, I think, then catch myself. In one week, I've become a thief and a sneak, and I've lied more times than I have in years. I don't know how to feel about that.

Peeve hits the sidewalk with his usual energy, busting me out of my thoughts. I make him sit for a few minutes, trying to figure out what, exactly, I plan to do, now that I've set myself free. I close my eyes and breathe, trying to see if I can make that under-the-skin bubbly feeling happen again. It doesn't, but a picture of Central Park fills my mind, so I call that a clue and get us walking.

We quick walk for several blocks and then, to the left, I spy a small opening in the fence. We slip into the park onto a paved pathway with benches lining one side. Instantly, my breathing changes and my spirits lift. I know the path leads to a section called Strawberry Fields, a memorial to John Lennon, one of the Beatles, who was killed before I was born. My mom used to love this place, partly because her mom loved John Lennon, and I realize it's been a really long time since I've been here. Tears come back again, and I'm not sure why. Maybe because I haven't even been letting myself miss her anymore.

I swat them away, not willing to let my sadness touch this place. It's too special, my favorite spot for thinking and dreaming. Usually people walk the path and sit on the benches, tourists mostly, but also some local artists and other folks, but today, nobody seems to be around. It's so strange.

As we approach the giant sparkling black and white mosaic tile-work circle with the word IMAGINE in the center, in honor of one of John's most famous songs, I'm struck by the word in a completely new way. The letters almost seem to be calling me, "CORAL... IMAGINE... CORAL..."

I stop in front of the circle, make Peeve sit, and then close my eyes. The letters keep calling, like a wind-whisper tickling my ear. Images float in my mind, though I feel them more than see them—an endless stretch of trees, waterfall mist, baked earth, troubled skies. For a minute, it seems like my body lifts off the ground, like waves of air flutter beneath me. At first, it's amazing, but then I get scared and force my eyes open.

Planted by my side, Peeve looks up at me, one ear cocked. When I smile at him, he gives a little whine, like he wants me not to do that anymore. "We're good, boy," I tell him. "I know it's been a weird day, but we're good."

"Do your parents know you're here?"

I startle and look behind me. An older woman, sporting a librarian bun and a thick sweater, stands a few feet back, her eyes dark and concerned. My first thought is to ask why she's dressed like its winter, but I know that's not my business. One more odd thing for the list.

"It's okay. I come here a lot," I tell her.

"I'm not sure that's a good idea."

Flashing a big smile, I try something else. "Plus, I have my big bodyguard." I hold up Peeve's leash.

The woman nods. "He looks like a good protector, but you're still young to be out here fending for yourself."

Fending for myself? Can't I just be walking in the park? Did the mayor issue a city-wide protection order for me or something? "We're good," I snap. "I've been taking care of myself for a long time now."

Her eyes narrow as she looks Peeve and me up and down, then she gives me a sad smile. "Well, you should probably head on home before too long. Don't want your parents to be concerned."

All I can do is purse my lips and nod. It makes sense for her to say parents, but it hurts just the same. Tears building for what feels like the millionth time, I give her a little wave and walk Peeve away from the memorial.

We keep going until we come to the lake, which is usually surrounded by a great carpet of the greenest grass providing a lush picnic and play space but looks like a burnt field of dry straw today. Still, I find a stick for Peeve and let him have fun for a while. When his tongue starts to loll, I sit us down on the prickery grass and pour some water into the cap of my bottle, so he can have a drink. I guzzle some myself and, when we've finished what we have, I settle him beside me and pull the compass out of my pocket.

"I need to figure out how this thing works, Peeve." He cocks his head and watches me.

"I mean, I don't really even know how to use a compass, but at least the north, south, east, and west stuff makes some sense."

Peeve chuffs and puts his big paw on my leg. Maybe he just wants me to stop complaining. I scratch his head and then pull the compass close, trying to see something new in the symbols. Mostly, they still look like squiggles, though I guess, if I squint, I can see a few differences.

One looks kind of like a cloud, maybe with rain in it. Another is more like a thin, arched cloud, shaped like a bridge or a rainbow. The third one is a whole circle, so maybe a ring of some sort? And the last one, the smallest one, looks like a wedge of the circle with a pointy top. A raindrop, I decide, whatever that means, suddenly remembering Miriam's riddle 'you will be the drops that create a wave of change.'

I look up, thinking about clouds, and it occurs to me that maybe I'm supposed to point the thing *at* the clouds. Maybe the sky matters. Or the horizon. I sigh. Or the sun. Or the grass. Or the ocean. How in the world am I supposed to know?

Feeling dumb, I hold it up anyway, not knowing what else to do. For the first time, I realize that nothing moves when I move it. There's a needle, but it stays still, no matter what I do. Doesn't the needle on a regular compass move?

A little chill slides across my neck. What if it's broken? Or, even worse, what if I broke it? What if I finally got something related to my mother and I ruined it?

If a feeling could make a sound, mine would be a snap, a break—of heart, of hope, of spirit. I'm lost. For a little while, I thought I got a gift. But now this day just feels like it's making fun of me.

Peeve whimpers, like he always does when he can tell I'm upset. He scooches his body closer and lays his head on my thigh. I rub his sweet head and try not to cry. That's not going to fix any of this.

"I just wish I knew what I'm supposed to do," I say, looking down at the compass.

My hand warms beneath the compass. I lift my hand to pick it up to look underneath, then notice the needle is moving. Back and forth, back and forth, then around. Back and forth, back and forth, then around.

"Holy moley," I squeal. "It's working. Peeve, it's working!!"

But Peeve has already noticed. He's sitting up, staring out at the lake like there's a boatload of T-bone steaks out there. I pat his neck, and it gives me a little jolt to feel how tense he is. What in the world?

I look out at the water too, then back at the compass, which now almost burns my skin as the needle moves faster and faster. I tap the face of the compass, more curious than I can ever remember. Beside me, Peeve snorts and leans forward, though his ears still lay low and relaxed. He's not worried, I tell myself, as a strange roaring sound surrounds us.

I follow Peeve's gaze, and then my eyes almost fall out of my head. Somehow, the lake is changing. As we watch, the water rises, first in a huge puff like a train's smokestack, and then thinning into a tube. It stretches way up into the air, almost like it means to touch the sky. I can't even gasp. I can't even think.

In my hand, the compass starts to jump. Up and down. Up and down. Then a wobble. Up and down. Up and down. Then a wobble. Faster and faster it jumps.

I watch, afraid to touch it, until Peeve rises to a stand next to me. Pulse leaping faster than the compass, I make myself look out at the water again. "Oh. Em. Gee," I murmur. I want to rub my eyes, because they can't be working right, but I also don't want to miss anything.

The shimmering blueish-golden tube bends toward us, flattening like a giant dog tongue at our feet. Peeve barks, just once, and I reach for him, securing his leash in that hand while I clamp down on the compass with the other. I can feel the water pulling us forward, slurping at my toes, sucking at my ankles.

"Hold on, boy," I scream. The water's pull is the strongest thing I've ever felt, like it's bonding with my body from the inside, drawing me into itself and tugging me onto what now looks like a massive bridge.

Peeve barks again, and I hope that means he understands, that he's okay, that *we're* okay. I want to reach out and pat him, but my arms feel glued to my side. My whole body feels different – as if I am liquid, merging with the water. I make one more wish, for a soft landing, and then whoosh! The water sweeps us away.

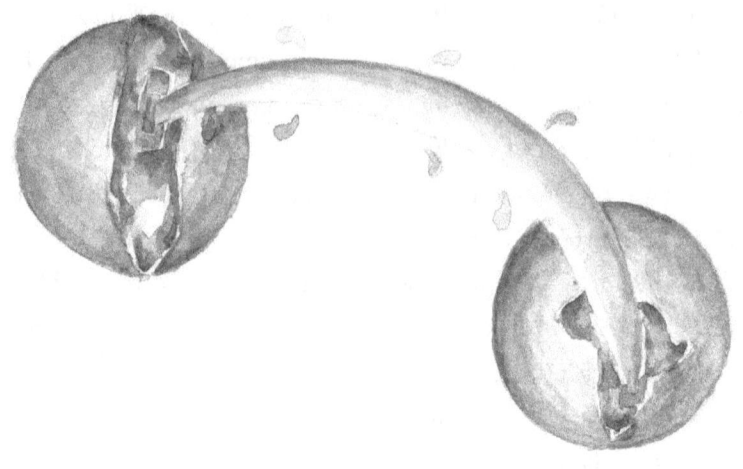

Chapter Eight

"Oof!" I land on my side, hard enough to cause a dusty poof in every direction. Through the dirty cloud, I see nothing but wide, deserted land and muted, rusty colors.

Not quite a soft landing, I think and rub my shoulder. But at least we survived. I hug Peeve first thing, never so happy to see his furry face. "What in the world was that?"

He sniffs me and licks my cheek, clearly enjoying the water still cascading down my face.

"Thanks, buddy." I swipe at my face, then glance down at my sopping clothes and the three-foot puddle surrounding us on the dusty ground. Here and there, patches of grass grow, but mostly, I just see lots of red dirt in every direction. How did we go from so much water to none at all? This can't be New York, I think, a little wave of panic starting to quiver in my gut. Where the heck are, we?

Peeve's ears prick up and he looks out into the distance. I squint that way and think I see movement. "Are there people over there, boy? Should we go look?"

He chuffs and rises to his feet.

"Only one way to find out where we are, right?" I say in my bravest voice. I lead him forward, but my stomach gets queasier with every step. I'm thinking that whoever said to be careful what you wish for really knows what she's talking about.

But I'm here, wherever that is. And it doesn't look like anyone's going to come and find me. I reach down and press my hand over my pocket, making sure I still have the compass. I don't feel the warmth anymore, but it's there, and I breathe a gigantic sigh of relief. I'm pretty sure I need it to get home. Now I just need to figure out what actually makes it work.

We walk for a while, and then I start to hear what Peeve's ears must have picked up long ago. Kids. I hear laughing and yelling, even some singing. My chest feels a little fuller at the sound. It's amazing how good it feels to not be alone, no matter where you are.

I expect to see a playground at some point, since that's what they sound like where I come from. When we get close, though, it's just more field with a rickety looking fence around it. Kids with chocolate brown colored skin which seems to beam with determination, run and play. Some chasing a frayed, dirty soccer ball and others playing tag, jumping rope, singing, or just talking. Some wear ragged, loose-fitting clothes, but others wear what must be school uniforms, short-sleeved white shirts and royal blue trousers or skirts. Most are shoeless.

Peeve gets excited when he sees them playing, and his steps get a little bouncier. "Easy, boy," I tell him. He's a big guy, and people sometimes get scared of him, so I sure don't want to rush in and cause a problem. "Before we do anything, we need some answers."

As if summoned by my request, a tall, thin girl about my age walks slowly toward us. I notice that her hair is shaved close to the head, like a buzz cut. That's different for a girl our age. She looks a little scared, and I try to imagine what we must look like to her, a soaking-wet white girl and a baby horse of a dog. I smile and give a little wave, hoping that will help, and also hoping I don't look as freaked out as I feel. I mean, there's really no way to be chill about what just happened, but I have to try.

"Hello," I say when she's a few feet away. "Can you tell me where we are?"

She blinks a few times, like she's not believing her eyes, but then her wide, welcoming smile appears. "This is Africa, my dear," she tells me. "Our country is called Malawi, and my name is Hope. You are welcome here."

My head buzzes. How is this possible? I was just in Central Park minutes ago. "Africa? Malawi??! But how did we get here?"

Next to me, Peeve wears his friendly face, although the height of his ears tells me he's a bit freaked out too. I pat him gently, needing to reassure us both. There has to be a good explanation for this.

50

The girl shakes her head slowly, and I can tell she doesn't quite trust her eyes. "I cannot tell you that, friend. You simply appeared."

My mouth falls open. "Holy cow! So, we just frickin' beamed from New York to Africa on a water bridge?"

Hope stares at me like I'm crazy, and I start to feel like I am. I take a deep breath, then sigh it out slowly. At least it's not as humid as it was in New York.

She walks in the other direction and waves for me to come along. I don't want to be rude, so I gather up Peeve's leash and hurry to her side. "Here we are," she says as we approach a round cement platform with a water pump in the center. "You look like you need this."

Peeve runs straight to the spout, darting in front of a long line of people, many of whom are brightly dressed women with babies and small children on their backs, who all look either stunned or worried. I yank him back and get in line with Hope, trying to smile an apology at every face along the way. Is this the only water source for all of these people? My cheeks color a little, thinking about not having to do more than turn the faucet in my own house for my entire life.

When it's finally our turn, Peeve rushes forward and laps like he's never seen water before. When I hear gasps from behind, I gently pull him back, worried that we broke some kind of rule. There definitely aren't any other dogs waiting in the water line.

Smiling her approval, Hope pumps a little more, and I drink through cupped hands, marveling at how good the water tastes. As my thirst goes away, questions fill my head, and the weight of the situation hits me like a ton of bricks. This is all pretty fantastic and unbelievable, but the idea of not being able to get home makes me feel wobbly and small.

I stare out at the horizon and try to pull myself together. The sun hangs low in the sky. "Do you know what time it is?" I ask Hope.

"It is after six, since that is when I gather water for my family each night."

My whole body shakes. Oh my God, my Dad is NOT going to be happy. He doesn't even know I'm out for a walk, never mind that I got myself lost in Africa.

"Why do you look so afraid, my dear? You have nothing to fear from us."

Her kindness calms me down, and I find a smile for her. "I'm more worried about how to get back home and how much trouble I'm going to be in if I figure it out."

Hope frowns. "Where is home?" she asks. "And may I know how you are called?"

I blink at her. How I'm *called*? I dig for my phone, then stop when it hits me that she's talking about my name. Here I am, slurping water and asking questions like I own the place, and I haven't even introduced myself. "Sorry," I say, finding her a big smile. "My name is Coral, and this big guy is my dog, Peeve."

Hope starts to smile, but it wavers a little when she glances at Peeve. "He is always friendly?"

"Oh, always," I tell her, a little confused. "He really loves people, and he's more like a big teddy bear than anything else." She doesn't quite look convinced, so I try harder. "He snores a little, so I sometimes make him sleep at the foot of my bed, but he's the best ever to snuggle with."

Her eyes get round. "This dog is bigger than most of our cows. He lives in your house?" "Of course," I say, not sure why that's so surprising. "He's part of my family."

Hope nods slowly, eyes on Peeve. "I am thinking you do not live in Africa?"

I shake my head. That's an understatement! "I live in New York City."

Her eyes narrow, and I can't tell if she doesn't know where that is or if she just doesn't believe me. I probably wouldn't believe me either. "It's in the United States," I add, glancing around me and wondering what it would be like to live surrounded by so much open land and shades of reddish brown. Sure, it goes a little flat and gray in New York City in the winter, but then spring comes to change things up. Hopefully that happens here too.

She presses her lips into a soft line, almost a smile. "I have heard of New York City, and I have studied America. I know it is very far away. Why are you here?"

I lean down to pump a little more water for Peeve, who's panting like there's not enough air in the world to satisfy him. "I can't actually explain that at the moment," I say, then realize the line has turned into a crowd and it's gathered around us.

Heart pounding, I grab hold of Peeve's collar as he drinks, hoping he'll act like the teddy bear I just described even when surrounded by what seems like at least five-hundred curious kids and their not-so-thrilled moms. Their bright eyes search me like I'm a ghost, and I take a long, deep breath. I've gone thirteen years with almost nothing interesting happening in my life and now, in just one day, I'm racking up one crazy, amazing moment after another.

Hope steps forward and holds out her hand. "Come with me," she says. "Let's talk."

I move toward her, but Peeve hesitates. "It's okay, boy," I say, reaching down to scratch his head. "I know I've asked a lot of you today, but hang in there with me, okay?"

He snorts then chuffs, which I take as a concerned yes.

"I know. You're right. But we do need to figure out how to get home."

He snorts again, then steps up and nudges my leg. He's such a good guy, I think, then glance at Hope, who now looks like she's not sure she wants to go anywhere with me. "He's just looking out for me," I tell her.

She breaks into a bright smile and holds out her hand once again. I hurry to take it this time.

She leads us across a nearby road and gestures toward a big rock at its edge. She sits down when we reach it, and I happily do the same. The sweet smell of burning charcoal mixed with dust washes over me, sharpened by thick exhaust from a wave of vehicles beeping their horns and zipping past us. I sneeze hard, my nose suddenly congested. I guess, even in Africa, traffic is a problem, but it never makes me stuffy at home.

I think about what I might want to ask her, then realize I have some urgent personal business to take care of first. "Hope, I know we have a lot to talk about, but before we do, can you tell me where to find a bathroom?"

She cocks her head, looking a little like Peeve when he's confused. "A bathroom?"

Oh, great. My heart flutters. This isn't good. "I need to, you know... use the toilet."

Her eyes light up, telling me she gets it, but then her lips purse like there's a problem. "Can you hold it for a while, Coral? There is no safe place near here for girls our age. If you want, I will take you to my home and you can go there."

A little wave of panic washes over me, like it might be a bad thing to move too far from the field where Peeve and I landed. But then I decide that I can't hold it forever, and Hope will know how to get back here if that's the only way home. "Okay," I say and we're off and moving again.

"I'm sorry we must walk a while, Coral, but water here is precious, and you will soon see that our toilets are not always worth visiting, especially for girls. So many of us fall sick." Her expression turned sad. "I have heard about sanitation and hygiene classes held many kilometers from my village, and I hope my mother will let me travel there. My little brother is one who is ill, and I really want to help him and others in our village, but my mother thinks I should spend my time working or taking care of my brother and sisters."

As I listen, guilt slithers up my spine and settles on my shoulders. In my house, we have three big bathrooms for just two people, plus someone who comes in once a week to clean them. "Do you think your mother will change her mind?"

She shakes her head. "She thinks I've lost *my* mind. I will have to wake before dawn to fill the water can, gather firewood, and fetch beans from the garden before I go, but I fear missing the information more than getting in trouble."

My guilt deepens. I mean, I know we have some problems in New York City, but my life couldn't be more different than Hope's. "It sounds like your days are long," I tell her.

She shrugs. "My family shares a vegetable garden with a few others in the village, and I am often asked to assist with the planting and harvesting. I am known for having a special ability to make things grow. Most days, I make it to school on time or close to it, but on the day of the assembly, I will have to miss school and walk much farther to learn about water related disease. But it will be worth it to help my brother and make it so fewer of us get sick."

"Wow." It's all I can say.

After we walk for a while, the area starts to look more like a neighborhood, with small structures made of wood and cardboard, curvy metal panels fixed on top. Children play outside, and the smell of food stirs hunger pangs. Peeve notices too, and I see him lick his chops.

"This is my home," Hope tells me. "The toilet is just there." She points to a wooden box about the size of a porta-potty behind the house. "We can tie Peeve's lead to the fence. I will get some water for him."

I watch her go, stunned at her generosity. I now understand what a gift that water is, especially when she's offering it to my dog instead of her family.

Feeling humble, and with a bladder ready to burst, I head to the wooden toilet box. Inside, I find a smelly hole in the ground with a bench above it, flies buzzing around everywhere. The sight grosses me out, but I have to go so badly I can't wiggle my way out of my sweaty shorts fast enough. At this point, pretty much any place would be okay.

"Ahhhhhh," I sigh, happy to have at least one worry off my mind.

As I leave the latrine, I plaster a smile on my face, not wanting Hope to see anything but gratitude. She joins me in the yard with three little kids, two girls and a boy. "Coral, these are my sisters, Patience and Rose, and this is my brother, Chiwembe, the youngest in our family. He has had many bouts with dehydration because of diarrhea. That's why I must attend the hygiene and sanitation workshop."

I nod, looking around for a sink and wondering what I should do if there's not one. "Could I maybe rinse my hands somewhere?"

Hope raises an eyebrow, like she's intrigued, then walks over and grabs a pitcher sitting near the house. She waves me over and gestures for me to hold out my hands. I rinse them, then wipe them on my shorts, trying not to make too big a deal of it and making a mental note to bring some soap back with me if I ever manage to first, get home, and second, come back to Malawi. In fact, I probably have tons of things at home that would blow her mind. My own brain explodes with the thought of how life-changing that class will be for her.

Then the wheels in my head turn faster, reminding me that I'd traveled to this place on a water bridge, reminding me that Miriam told me I would soon meet three other girls my age, reminding me that I'd come here from a city having water problems of its own. It feels like electricity pulsing beneath my skin. "Hope, I don't know exactly how I got here, but I think there's a reason you and I needed to meet. There are water problems in New York, too. And I spent my day getting this mysterious gift and meeting this strange woman who told me I'm Pathfinder of the Ecomasters and have a mission to find three other girls my age."

Hope stares at me, eyes narrow. Her hand rises to her neck, and she presses her fingers against the collar of her blouse. "What is this gift?"

I take a deep breath and pull the compass from my pocket. "It showed up at my door this morning." I hold it out to her.

Cradling it in her palm, Hope peers at its face. "What do these symbols mean?"

"I don't know," I tell her with a shrug. "I didn't even think it worked until right before I landed here. It's not a normal compass, that's for sure."

Her dark eyes fix on mine. "And you say it just showed up at your door?"

"Yes. With a note. Leading me to a lady named Miriam who was nice but left me with more questions than she answered."

"She called you a Pathfinder?"

My breath catches in my throat, and Hope's forehead creases like she's solving an algebra problem. "That's the word she used," I tell her.

She purses her lips and says nothing for what feels like a long time. Finally, she lifts her hand to her neck again, then reaches beneath her collar and holds up a pale blue pendant carved to look like a flower. "I found this outside my door a few days ago. It is a lotus blossom, the flower of my country and a symbol of purity, carved from Malawi agate, which is very rare. No one I know owns such a thing."

I gasp, loud enough to make Peeve jump to his feet and walk to my side. He noses the back of my knee like he's checking for weak spots. "It's okay, buddy," I tell him, never taking my eyes off Hope and the pendant. "Was there a note?"

She nods. "It said my name on one side." "Anything on the other side?"

Hope nods again. "It said, 'The world in a wish.'"

A long shiver scurries down my spine like a centipede in a big hurry. I don't know why hearing this message rattles me more than the giant water bridge, but it sure the heck does. "Did you?" I ask.

"Did I what?"

"Wish."

She looks up at the sky, eyes in thinking mode, then nods. "After my mother said I should do my chores instead of going to the assembly, I made a wish to help my people. I remember falling asleep with that thought. This was wrapped in cloth and lying outside my door the next morning."

My mouth falls open. This is crazy. Kind of exciting, but super crazy. "That's what made the compass work too. A wish."

Hope's eyes get big and wide. "How is that possible?"

"I don't know yet." The words sound sadder than I mean them, which makes Peeve lick my hand. I scratch under his chin, needing him to stay calm while I figure things out. "I guess we'll find the answers as we go."

She studies me, not quite looking convinced. "So, we will see each other again?" "None of this makes sense if we don't."

Hope nods. "You are right, Pathfinder Coral," she says and then smiles, and we shall learn the way of the Ecomasters.

Just then, a familiar sound blasts out of my pocket. I jump at least a foot in the air, making Peeve bark and dance at my side. "My phone,"

I tell her as I try to pull it out of my pocket and calm my canine friend at the same time. When I finally see the screen, it feels like every drop of blood in my body lands in my shoes. The word 'Dad' glares at me. "Yikes," I say, exhaling hard as I push the 'ignore' button.

"You have a phone just for you?"

"Yeah. You don't?" I look up at Hope, and the amazement on her face makes me feel silly. Of course, she doesn't have a phone. She doesn't even have soap, for crying out loud. "Sorry," I say. "That just popped out. I forgot how far away from home I am."

She beams at me with her big smile, and I know I've been forgiven.

"I guess I do need to get back there. That call means my Dad is looking for me."

"Why did you not answer?"

I sigh. "It's a long story. I'm sure we'll get to talk about it sometime." I look her in the eye. "Now that we're friends, that is."

Her smile gets even bigger. "I am very happy about this."

"Me too," I say. "Okay, but how will we get home." Hope reflects with furrowed brows, "Coral, if we think about how things have happened so far, it looks like you need to be near water, and make a wish with the compass."

Yes, that's exactly right, I enthusiastically agree. But Hope adds "Water is harder to find here."

I sigh. "So, I've seen." I glance down at Peeve, who's no longer dancing around but definitely not relaxed. He's panting again, which makes me think of how he looked when we first got to Malawi. "That's it," I say. "The pump. We need to go back to that pump." That'll be much easier to find than the random puddle we landed in first.

Her eyes light up. "Good thinking. I forgot to fetch my family's water, so it will also help me finish my chores."

We dash off the way we came, Hope and Peeve and me, and within minutes, we're back on the cement platform. Hope grabs the pump handle and looks at me. "Ready?"

"One sec." I run over and hug her, then look into her friendly eyes. "Thank you for being so kind and teaching me so much. I promise I will find a way for us to stay in touch."

She nods and squeezes my hand. "Yes, you will. Today, I learned that anything is possible."

My stomach goes a little queasy at that, since 'anything' doesn't just mean the good stuff. Enough of that, I tell myself, and steer Peeve closer to the spout. I pull the compass from my pocket, give Hope one more smile, and stare down into the needled face. "I wish to go home," I say as Hope's hand goes into motion and the water starts flowing.

Peeve whines a little, like he's seen this movie this before and wasn't a fan, but I tug him closer and keep staring at the compass. Just like last time, the needle starts to do its thing. First, there's the back and forth pattern and then, just as the tugging pressure starts in my rib cage, the needle spins faster and faster.

I hear a sharp snort from Peeve, and I look up just in time to see the water swell as it leaves the pump. In a second or two, it's somehow a river, foamy with rapids. It doesn't touch Hope, standing behind the pump, but makes a channel big enough to swallow Peeve and me. The rapids catch us, making me feel like I'm first in line at a water park as it sweeps us off the platform and across the field.

Though I try to keep my eyes open, to really see how this all works, water rushes from every direction, and like before, I feel as if I'm turning to liquid, too. I'm flopping, bobbing, sailing; fighting for all I'm worth to hold onto Peeve's leash. And then, with a giant splash and a muffled thump, I land and Peeve tumbles on top of me.

"Whoa, boy," I yell, trying to push his giant hind end off my belly. I settle him next to me and pat his neck, then look up and realize we're sitting in the fountain in the lobby of my apartment building.

"Oh, man." I jump to my feet, thinking about the universe of trouble I'll be in if Mr. Dobbins spots us. He takes his job VERY seriously, almost like he built the building himself. And after the texts my Dad sent, complaints from Mr. Dobbins would only make things worse.

"C'mon, Peeve." I tug his leash and make him follow me out of the fountain. We squish toward the elevator and I push the button, all the while staring at the front door and mapping our escape to the stairwell if Mr. Dobbins looks our way. When the ding sounds, I hold my breath, wait a million seconds for the doors to open, and run us inside. Then I pound the 'close door' button over and over, mostly just making myself feel better. I don't breathe again until the elevator starts moving.

On our floor, we slosh our way through the hallway. I listen at the door before I put my key in the lock, but everything sounds as quiet as always. I step inside, take off my shoes, and trot Peeve and me down the hall and into my bathroom. I dry us both off and change into my bathrobe, one ear tuned for my Dad's grumbling and stomping. Nothing happens, though, which makes me almost as nervous as relieved. What's going on?

When I finally tiptoe out and look for him, I find the apartment empty. He's not anywhere—not his office or his bedroom or even in the shower. My heart starts to gallop a little. He might have been a jerk today, but he's still my Dad.

I creep into the kitchen, super confused, and I find a note on the counter.

IN A MEETING AT MY OFFICE. CALLING POLICE IF YOU'RE NOT HERE WHEN I FINISH. PHONES ARE MEANT TO BE ANSWERED. WE'LL DISCUSS AT DINNER.

I gulp, now nervous and relieved for completely different reasons. At least I didn't have to face him when I walked through the door. Though I can barely think with the sound of my scared pulse in my ears, an idea does break through, and it feels like a pretty good option.

Flipping his note over, I write one of my own.

SORRY, DAD. PEEVE NEEDED ANOTHER WALK AND YOU WERE BUSY. NOT HUNGRY. SEE YOU IN THE MORNING.

I almost add something about my phone, that it was dead, or I forgot it, but I just can't make myself write the lie. After today, I already have a lot to answer for, and WAY too many secrets. Crossing fingers that my Dad will feel as tired as I do by the time, he gets home, I grab a bag of chips and a banana and head to my room. All those miles between here and Africa are starting to catch up with me.

Chapter Nine

My Dad's in the shower when I go looking for him in the morning, which feels like the luckiest thing ever. I sure don't need him yelling at me again, like he did when he got home last night. I mean, I know it seems to him like I'm suddenly running down at bad path at top speed, but honestly, I feel like I could accuse him of the very same thing. Thank goodness I didn't do that last night, since that would have ruined today for sure.

I decide to keep up this note-writing thing—something HE started; I tell myself—since that seems like the best way to out of the house again today. I'm sure not going to miss a chance to see what else this compass can do. Yesterday, Africa...today, who knows?!

Knowing I don't have much time, I brush my teeth, throw on some clothes, get Peeve some food, and write my note while he eats. I feel a little bad with this message, since I know it's not going to make my Dad happy. But then I think about yesterday, about the way he talked to me, and my backbone gets a little stronger.

MORNING, DAD. HAD TO TAKE PEEVE OUT. BACK SOON. MY PHONE IS CHARGED.

I smile at that last sentence. Technically, I'm being honest. My phone IS charged at this very minute. I'm not promising to answer it, and I'm not making excuses about yesterday, and yet it somehow sounds like I've covered it all.

"I can be pretty smart sometimes, can't I, boy?"

Peeve looks up at me and licks his jowls. Clearly, he agrees. "You finished?"

He chuffs and puts his nose back in the bowl, then immediately lifts it again. His ears seem to flop in disappointment.

Since the lake worked yesterday, it makes sense to go back again today. Water is key, that much I know so far, and if I'm going to find these other two girls, I might as well make use of the biggest body of water in my neighborhood.

Spirits high and hopeful, at least if I don't think about how angry things are at home, I try to focus on my mission as Pathfinder. It's another hot day and I feel like the city is trying not to breathe or move any more than necessary. I can definitely see more homeless people than usual and even a few kids which is basically unheard of in my neighborhood. The hot dog vendors all have signs that read "NO WATER" If that's not bad enough, I realize that I forgot my own bottle. Urghhh! If it's going to be like this every day, this might actually be the year I'm happy to see summer end... if it even does.

We get to Strawberry Fields in about fifteen minutes, but I walk right past it today and head for the lake. Peeve barks at me when we get to the shore, expecting to play fetch like yesterday, but I don't even look for a stick.

"Sorry, boy, but we have important things to do."

I swear he frowns.

"I know. You're bummed. And if this compass doesn't work this time, I promise I'll find you the biggest, juiciest stick in the park."

Peeve sighs, like only a saintly best friend can, then lowers his body onto the straw-like grass and stares at me.

"Thanks, buddy. You're the best."

I flop down next to him and quickly eat the almonds and string cheese I brought for myself. I have no idea what's going to happen this time, so it's probably better to have something in my stomach. Since he's being so chill, I toss Peeve a couple of treats too. When we both finish chewing, I throw away my garbage, try to get in the same spot at yesterday, and call Peeve to my side.

Taking a deep breath, I pull the compass from my pocket and stare down into its face. I shake it, but the needle doesn't move, not even a bit. "I wish I understood what you want," I say, then roll my eyes at myself. *It's a compass, not a person, Coral.* But deep down, I'm not so sure *what* it is. Maybe my mom's spirit is trapped in there or something.

The heat starts in my palm, and this time I'm happy to feel it. At this point, I can't imagine much worse than finding out the magic's run out. I close my fingers around its face, feeling the jump of the needle this time, and then the steady build as it spins faster. I stare out into the water.

Next to me, Peeve sits calmly, like he's totally ready. I reach down and grab his collar as the water starts to bubble and rise. As the gaping water mouth stretches itself into a massive bridge once again, I lean into the pull. I want to pay better attention today, to notice more when I'm in the wave.

But it's no use. Before I can summon a thought or even blink, I'm hitting bottom once again. I feel something hard beneath me, then wetness up to my armpits. Peeve sneezes, sending a burst of lake water and dog drool into my ear and across my cheek.

"Dude!" I swipe at my face and scowl at him, but he looks so rattled that I feel bad. "Thanks for being a good sport, buddy." I lean over to kiss his neck, then glance around me and try to figure out where we landed this time.

Another fountain. This one is much bigger, in the middle of a city square, with a smaller, fruit bowl-looking thing at its center. People are everywhere, walking and talking and enjoying the day, and it feels like at least half of them are staring at the soaking wet girl and her dog in the middle of their monument. Yikes!

"Let's go, boy," I say to Peeve. He only moves his eyes at first, peering up at me like he's not completely sure I should be calling the shots. "I know, I know. But let's make sure we don't get arrested, okay?"

He stands and shakes himself again. I put my arms up and turn away, then realize I really can't be more soaked than I am now. When he finishes, I choose the direction with the smallest number of bystanders, then steer us up and over the side of the fountain and onto the sidewalk. Though I'm pretty sure we're not in Africa this time, I can't tell much more than that.

All around me, I see a strange mixture of modern buildings and dilapidated shack-style places. I can't read the signs, all written in a curly cue lettering I've never seen before. A fishy smell permeates my senses,

making me glad I took the time to eat before I got here. It doesn't exactly smell bad, but if that's what's for lunch, I might pass.

I better not still be here at lunchtime, I think. Even if I don't understand the big picture yet, I do know I don't have time to waste. And every step I take will hopefully get me that much closer to finding my mom. That part sure can't come soon enough!

A second later, I jump as an ancient-looking Asian woman appears right in front of my face. Her stark white braid reaches almost to her knees, and it looks like she's been sleeping in her crumpled tan tunic. She bows toward me, her hands pressed together like she's praying. I notice she's leaning on a crooked stick to stay upright, and I step between her and Peeve, just in case he gets any ideas about being 'friendly.'

"Hello ma'am. My name is Coral," I say.

Shoulders hunched, the woman leans forward and looks at me with such kind eyes. I gasp to see a flicker of blue-gold light at their center. "Sabai dee," she says.

Uh-oh. I swallow hard. What if no one understands me here? Miriam didn't mention anything like that. I try to smile, but something suddenly feels very wrong, like when you pop one of those giant, convenience store gumballs machine in your mouth, then worry it's going to roll down your throat and choke you before your jaws can crack its shell.

The woman's smile stretches wide. She takes a small step back and, in less than a blink, a young girl appears beside her, right out of thin air. She has the same blue-gold eyes. "You look worried, Coral," the girl says to me.

Every muscle in my body relaxes when I realize she's speaking English. Thank goodness! That would have been a disaster.

She holds out her hand. "I am Phonepasit. I do not know how you got here, but I am happy to meet you." Just like the old woman, she beams with loving kindness. I admire her red blouse, tucked neatly into a long navy skirt with a pretty gold trim at the bottom. Her dark black hair, tied neatly in a ponytail, lays across one shoulder.

"Where are we?" I ask, pulling a curious Peeve back before he gets drool all over Phonepasit's shoes.

"This is Vientiane, the capital city of the Lao People's Democratic Republic, but you may call it Laos for short. You are welcome here."

Wow. First Africa, and now Asia. Miriam wasn't kidding about this adventure thing. I shiver, thinking about how much cooler it is here than in New York, and then I remember that I'm also drenched.

The old woman places a hand on Phonepasit's shoulder, and they nod at each other before the woman walks away. Phonepasit looks back at me. "Can I offer you some dry clothes, Coral? You must be cold. Why did you and this dog go swimming in Nam Phou Fountain?"

I chuckle, not sure what to say. "It's a long story, but I'll try to explain. Those dry clothes would be wonderful, though. Thank you."

Phonepasit smiles and bows. "Please come with me."

As we walk, I tell her that I'm from New York City, and that I'm pretty sure I was supposed to meet her. She nods like she understands completely.

After a few minutes, she opens a big blue metal door set into a long wall of concrete. We step inside and my mouth drops open. We're standing in a magical garden with huge golden statue centered between a square of small doors. "Wow, this is beautiful. Is that Buddha?" I ask.

"Thank you, Coral. That is a goddess of our Buddhist faith, Quan Yin. She is a very important part of life here. Now, are you hungry?"

I think about the strong fish smell from the square and start to shake my head, but she looks so friendly that I just can't say no. "A little," I say and cross my fingers that whatever she brings won't be gross.

"I will get you some clothes and, after you change, we can have sticky rice."

Sticky rice? That sounds harmless. I smile and nod, grateful for so much kindness, though also a little worried about spending so much time on clothes and food instead of figuring out why I'm here.

Phonepasit disappears behind a door, then soon returns with a tidy pile of clothes. My new outfit, almost identical to hers, has a short-sleeved white blouse and a navy skirt that falls below my knees. Instead of a golden band around the bottom, mine is multi- colored, like a rainbow!

When I appear in my clothes, Peeve circles and sniffs me for what feels like five minutes. "It's okay, boy," I tell him. "I don't have a fur coat like you do, so this feels better."

Phonepasit tilts her head and studies us. "He understands you?" I consider that. "I really think he does."

"He is also hungry?"

"He is always hungry!"

She grins. "We can take him to the chicken coop and feed him there. My grandmother will not want him at the table."

I bust out laughing. "He doesn't eat at the table at my house either. The chicken coop will be fine, thank you."

After we get Peeve settled, Phonepasit takes me to their kitchen. The old woman from the fountain bows and waves me closer. On the simple wood table, I see a big bowl of what must be the sticky rice. It looks like regular white rice we'd have at home, but she tells me it is actually a different type of plant and is cooked in a special way to make it sticky. I take small bites at first, but soon I'm eating as happily as Phonepasit and her grandmother.

After a few minutes, I decide it's time to learn what I can. "So, tell me about yourself, Phonepasit."

She smiles shyly and lowers her head. "I am not sure what you'd like to know."

"What makes you happy? What do you care about?"

That seems to do the trick. Beaming, she looks me in the eye. "Perhaps you will not believe this, but I have a special ability to transmit messages through the airwaves. After I discovered this, my friends and I decided to start producing a radio show. We visit communities with environmental challenges, like water scarcity or garbage pile ups, and then share their stories on the radio so people can learn how to improve their communities. This is the work I care about most."

I feel a huge smile crease my face. *Bingo.* This has to be why I'm here. "That's amazing," I tell her. "And now I know why I was supposed to meet you."

Her eyebrows dart toward her forehead. "You care about things like this?"

"Yes, I do. We have those same problems in my city, and I'm learning that it's part of my mission to do something about them."

Phonepasit grins and leans forward over her rice bowl. "My friends and I have some events planned for today. You would be most welcome if you'd like to join us, Coral."

"I'd love to go. Can I take Peeve?" Suddenly, the idea of leaving him behind makes me anxious. What if I beam someplace else by mistake and leave him here? I won't know how to get back for him.

Phonepasit sighs. "I don't think so," she says. "We have two stops to make, with many people to see, and I'm afraid not everyone here would be happy to see such a large dog. I hope you understand that it is not possible for Peeve to join us."

"Oh gosh. Of course, I understand," is all I can say. I seriously feel so nauseated and dizzy. The thought of leaving Peeve behind is almost too much to bear.

"Can we go tell him?" I ask quietly, and then an idea comes to me. "Or is there someone you trust we could leave him with?

"I cannot think of anyone who would stay with him, but I will go with you to let him know," she says, and something in her voice tells me it's not natural here to be so deeply attached to an animal.

Pulling myself together, I explain the situation to Peeve. He lies on the ground while I talk, looking a little downtrodden, but he doesn't bark or run after me. I'm honestly a little grateful for the chickens, hoping they'll keep him company. And before I walk away, I whisper a little promise that we'll be together again before he knows it. He peers up at me, sad but trusting, and my heart flutters, like it doesn't remember how to beat without him by my side.

As we squeeze into the back of an old minivan, I meet Phonepasit's friends, who are all about my age. "The first school we will visit today has been focusing on creative ways to recycle and reuse garbage like candy wrappers and juice boxes," Phonepasit tells me. "They will be hosting a fashion show, and we are going to watch."

"This is all so amazing," I say, meaning the fashion show and the radio show, but also all the magic that brought me here. "I can't wait to see the fashions. The city where I am from, New York, is known for fashion and shopping." I stop talking, realizing I sound so silly and shallow.

"That's so interesting, Coral. Would you mind if we interview you before the day is over?" asks the only boy in the group, Liko. I feel myself turn red, but the question also makes me feel better, like one of them.

"Sure, I'd love that," I tell him.

The fashion show is like nothing I'd ever seen before, dozens of outfits made with colorful scraps of paper. One girl walks out in a dress made of old CDs, held together by orange peels. Another presents a pink, green, and yellow-colored flower vase from juice box material that looks like origami I've seen in New York. Inside the vase stand light pink roses made of toilet paper. "This is so beautiful," I say. "Where do you guys get all of these bright papers?"

She smiles and looks thrilled to be asked. "Before we started the collection, people threw a lot of the stuff into the river. This caused so many problems for the fish, not to mention the flooded drains clogged with plastic bags when it rains. Of course, this is a small project, but we can already see smaller garbage piles in some places."

"That must make you feel really good," I say.

"We also collect water and soda bottles and use them for other designs. You will have to come back another day to see those."

"I will try," I tell her, smiling to myself about just how easy it's become for me to rush around the world.

Our next stop is the radio station where Phonepasit and her friend Suki record a two-minute advertisement to promote their upcoming show. I watch them, thinking how important it is for me to learn about this and that there just has to be some connection to the water situation back home.

"Phonepasit, maybe you can visit me in New York sometime and we can take to the airwaves together?"

"I would love that Coral, but I don't know how that would be possible."

I smile to myself again, the girl with the magical secret. "I might have a few ideas about that. So, tell me, why is the young radio producers' group so important to you?"

"So many kids our age, even my cousins and my friends, live without access to water for drinking or proper toilets to use. Even electricity is a luxury for some." She pauses and smiles. "But almost everybody here has a battery-operated radio. That is how I can reach them."

"That makes a lot of sense," I tell her.

"With my gift of transmitting messages through air, I figured out a practical way to communicate with people through the radio, then brought it to a lady I know in the government offices in Vientiane. She really liked it and agreed to help us get started."

Next, we drive for a long time, maybe an hour, maybe two, my perception of time seems to be off kilter, but it was great to have time to talk to all of Phonepasit's friends. Eventually, we stop at a school with gatherings of round straw huts nearby. I glance around, trying to take it all in. The children were dressed in tidy school uniforms, girls with their straight black hair tied neatly into ponytails, boys dressed as little men with shoes, navy trousers and white-collar shirts. Near the school, women (probably mothers and village dwellers) gather at the well to fetch water, and beyond the well sits a small altar with a large golden statue of the Buddha behind it.

"We are now in the province of Savannakhet," Phonepasit tells me. "This school is a participant in our Young Radio Producers network. We are here to conduct workshops and interview some people today."

I'm so impressed, and I want to ask a ton of questions but, before I can do that, the five young radio producers fan out around the school yard. Two of the girls pin posters to nearby trees, then each one stands silently beside the poster, hand raised. Phonepasit goes to the well where the women are gathered, and Suki joins several kids at the handwashing station near the latrines. Liko carries two heavy-looking boxes to a row of wooden benches and unpacks t-shirts, his tape recorder, and a microphone.

Rotating between the five stations, I learn an incredible amount about the transmission of germs from human and animal poop and touching unwashed raw food. A nudge to my conscience as I remember Peeve's giganto-size deposit that I accidently left on someone's grass back home. I promise myself to go back when I can and that it will *never* happen again.

My favorite part of all is the interview station. Liko asks the adults important questions like where their water comes from, where and how they cook, and the kinds of illnesses they've had to deal with, then records their answers for the radio program. Watching how smart and committed they all are to their communities makes me feel happy and hopeful, like I'm somehow exactly where I'm supposed to be.

Soon, it's time to go back to Phonepasit's home. As soon as we get there, I rush to the chicken coop and, with great relief, my eyes meet Peeve's. Still lying on the ground, though now circled by his new chicken friends, he lifts his head and wags his tail at me. I can't help running to him.

"There's my boy," I tell him and give him all the scratches and hugs he missed out on while I was gone.

Taking hold of his leash, I lead him out of the coop. His tail wags even harder. Though I had a great day, it's amazing how much better I feel to be back with Peeve.

When I look back at the house, I see Phonepasit standing just outside the door, smiling at me. She waves me over, and we sit together on a bench in the middle of her beautiful garden. The shining Quan Yin statue beams and somehow seems to approve of our meeting.

"How old are you, Phonepasit?" The question just pops out, now that it's just the two of us.

She blinks, clearly surprised. "I have just turned thirteen."

"Me too! And now I have another question, and it might sound a little strange." Phonepasit smiles, then gives a slow nod. "Please ask."

"Have you gotten any sort of surprise gift lately?"

She nods slowly.

"Did it come after you made a wish? And was there a note?"

Her eyes get so big they seem to take up most of her face. "How could you know that?"

Relief washes over me, and I exhale so hard I surprise myself. "It happened to me too," I tell her.

She leans closer. "What was your gift?"

For a second, I panic, since I haven't thought about the compass in hours. What if I lost it while I was traveling all over Laos? I pat my pocket, then exhale hard again. All good. "It's a compass, though not an ordinary compass."

"What does that mean?"

"It's probably better to show you than to try to explain, but I can't do that until it's time for me to leave."

Phonepasit looks a little scared, but she nods.

"What was yours?" I ask.

She reaches into her skirt pocket. "I carry it with me everywhere," she says and holds out a miniature version of the Quan Yin behind us. Also golden, and very lovely, it's small enough to fit in the palm of her hand. "It has even more meaning for me because this goddess is said to perceive the sounds and vibrations of the world."

"And the wish?"

"To find a better way to share my message."

For a second, my pulse feels a little fluttery, like I might not be ready for all of this. I mean, I'm only thirteen. We're all only thirteen. Honestly, I'm not completely sure I believed it was real before now. But now I've traveled across the world twice, and I've 'found' two girls my same age and in my exact situation, and everything is just the way Miriam said it would be. This is real. I really am a Pathfinder! And whatever that Ecomaster thing means is still a mystery to me. Seems like maybe I'm meant to find the path for all of us, but where? And why?

"Are you okay, Coral?" As she noticed that my daydreams were taking me away from her, Phonepasit puts a hand on my shoulder. I nod and smile. "Yeah, thanks. It all just hard to believe sometimes." "What is hard to believe?"

I tell her everything I know—about my wish, my note, Miriam, and Hope. I tell her, as best I can, about how the compass works, what the water does, and how I ended up in the fountain. Then I make the same promise I made to Hope, that I will find a way, once I get home, for us to stay in touch and see one another again. And at that moment, Phonepasit came closer and whispered a plan for our communication into my ear. I almost hit myself in the forehead thinking, of course! She's the Communicator, she already knows how to help us to stay in touch.

"What's even more amazing," I say as I wrap up my story, "is that both you and Hope speak English. Can you imagine if I plopped down in other countries and couldn't communicate with anyone?"

Phonepasit peers at me like she doesn't understand. "I do not speak English, Coral."

I just stare at her. I don't know what to say. "Then how are we talking?" I finally manage.

She giggles. "I thought you were speaking Lao."

Holy cow. How is that possible? How can my brain understand languages I've never even heard before? Eyes on Quan Yin, Phonepasit, seeming older than her years, quietly stated "it is the water which translates our languages. We are water and our world is water and all languages are held within the DNA of our world in every drop."

I rub my head, sort of wishing I could just massage these answers around my mind, and then it hits me. The compass definitely has something to do with water, and it can grant wishes and let me travel the world in water, so of course, it makes so much sense that it can turn our watery brains into a language translator too. I shake my head, wondering what I could have done to deserve this level of magic. As soon as the question appears, my mom's face lights up my thoughts, reminding me that, even if I'm in the middle of this adventure, it's not really about me or what I've done.

"I am glad you were brought here, Coral." Phonepasit pats my hand and beams at me.

I take a deep breath and let her smile sink in. "I am too, Phonepasit. Thank you for everything today, for feeding me and clothing me and teaching me. You've been a very good friend."

"Is it time for us to say goodbye?"

I sigh, trying hard not to think about how things will be when I get home. A frowning version of my Dad's face flashes in my mind, but I push it away. "I do need to get back," I say.

"And how do we do that?"

A chuckle rolls up and out of my throat. "Like I said, it's better if I show you. I think it might work best if we go back to the fountain."

Phonepasit laughs too, and then she stands. "Then I will take you there."

Next to me, Peeve gets to his feet. He presses his nose against my thigh and then looks up at me. I guess we're all in agreement.

When we reach the fountain, I take one last look at this amazing place. What a day! Then I turn to Phonepasit and pull her into a hug. "We'll see each other soon," I whisper.

She pats my back. "I look forward to it, Coral."

I look around me, hoping to have less of an audience this time, but no luck. People are everywhere. Ah, well. Can't stay here forever.

"C'mon, boy," I say to Peeve as I step over the side and into the fountain.

He chuffs and wags his tail, actually looking pleased to get in the water this time.

Once in place, I pull out the compass and squeeze it tight. "I wish I was back in my apartment," I say, hoping the right wording will keep me out of the lobby this time.

My eyes lock with Phonepasit's. She looks a little scared and a lot excited. I smile when the water starts to churn around my feet. I lift my hand to wave but, by the time my fingers move, Peeve and I are wrapped in a swirling cone of water.

Trying not to think about how much panic this sight might be causing in the city square around the fountain, I close my eyes and hope for the best, but then curiosity gets the best of me and I take a quick peek. Phonepasit rewards me with a Christmas morning-sized smile, while the people around her stare like a fleet of alien creatures just landed. I giggle, partly because of what I see, and partly because bubble jets seem to tickle me from head to toe.

The water pressure eases, going from full boil to calm, and I open my eyes just as my body flops down onto Peeve's. He's somehow still on his feet, and I'm somehow sprawled across his back, and we're somehow smack in the middle of his doggy shower in the laundry room. His doggy shower...really?

And then it hits me. This is good. This is very good. What better way to explain my current state of dampness than saying I was bathing Peeve? Way to go, compass!

Feeling like the clock is ticking, I jump out of the shower and run over to close the door. Then I dump some doggy shampoo on Peeve and rinse him with the still-squirting shower nozzle. After I dry him a little, I take off the clothes from Phonepasit and wrap myself in one of his giant-sized doggy towels. With a deep breath, I finally open the door and start the trek to my room.

As I walk, I make a list of all the places I could have been in the apartment and not have been seen—my room, bathroom, back terrace, and BINGO—doggy shower! I smile, feeling triumphant, until my conscience tugs at me. I shouldn't be lying to my Dad, but how can I possibly tell him about this?

Fortunately, I don't have to lie this time. There are no questions, just a few quick nods at Peeve and my wet hair, and then a reminder about the leftover Chinese food in the fridge as my Dad walks another anxious-looking businessperson into his office and closes the door. Whatever he's working on, it's crazy important to him.

Chapter Ten

When I wake up in the morning, after a quiet night spent with a long, warm bath, sweet and sour chicken, and doggy snuggles, I still can't believe my luck. Cautiously, I check my phone, half-expecting an angry text from my Dad. Instead, in about a second and a half, I go from feeling lucky to feeling like the worst friend in the world. I have three voicemails from Jasper. Three. He's probably either really annoyed or really worried by now.

I sit up in bed, trying not to disturb Peeve, and start listening to the messages. "Hey, where are you?" the first one says. "Did your Dad calm down? Is everything cool over there?"

I look at the time of that one and figure it came in just about when I landed in Malawi. Apparently, the signal's not as strong there. I listen to the next one, feeling guiltier by the moment. "Coral, call me back, okay? Unless he took your phone away or something. My mom said we can go back to the garden tomorrow if you want to come. Just call me and tell me what's up."

His voice does that squeaky thing again, making the last few words sound like a broken clarinet. My eyes flood a little, because I miss seeing him, and because I'm sad to hear how worried he sounds.

I try to piece together when his call might have come in, and I realize I might actually have been on a magical water bridge at the time. How in the world did I not call him as soon as I got home? Or even the next day? The most amazing thing that's ever happened to me, and I completely forget to call my best friend!

Feeling about as bad as a girl can feel, I throw back the covers and swing my feet onto the soft carpet. Peeve sits up and looks at me, clearly annoyed that I've disrupted his sleep. "Sorry, boy," I tell him. "I think it's time to get up."

He snorts his disagreement and buries his face in the comforter. I pat his side as I listen to the next message, wincing even before Jasper starts talking because I know he had to have been really annoyed, and probably worried, by the time he left this one.

"I don't know if you got my other messages," he says, his voice quiet and tired, like someone else is talking for him. "I hope you're okay. I know I said you could come over today, but I don't think that's going to work. I'm feeling kind of sick and gross, so you should probably just stay away."

My heart feels like it flops against my ribs. None of it matters anymore, since that was yesterday, but I'm still disappointed. And now, if Jasper's sick, it might be a while before I get a chance to see him. I stare at my feet, bummed to feel so bummed. At least I can call and make him feel better.

I dial his number, then pace the room as I wait for him to answer. His phone rings, way too many times, and then I leave him a voicemail. "Oh my gosh, Jasper. I am so sorry I didn't call sooner but man, do I have the best excuse EVER! I can't tell you over the phone, but as soon as you're better, I'm going to come to your house and blow your mind. Like, seriously. You will NOT believe what happened."

Just as I finish, there's a sharp knock on my door. Without even waiting for me to say anything, my Dad pokes his head in and studies me. "Who were you talking to?"

"Jasper. Well, Jasper's voicemail."

He narrows one eye and looks at me harder than I can ever remember. "And what's so important?"

A weird sensation creeps over me, halfway between mad and suspicious. "Who said it was?"

"I heard you, Coral. You said he wouldn't believe what happened."

My frown feels too big for my face, and I'll probably just get in trouble if he sees it, so I turn away from him and tug open one of my dresser drawers like I need to find something. "Why ask if you heard me?"

He steps inside the room. "Because I couldn't tell what you were talking about."

"And why does it matter?"

"Look at me, Coral."

The bite in his voice makes me jump a little. I peek over my shoulder, hoping he'll look like the Dad I'm used to.

"Turn around and look at me."

I close the drawer and face him, surprised to see him in a dark suit and bright red tie. He's been working at home so much I forgot how he used to dress for the office.

"You're my daughter. And I care about you. That means I care about what you're up to."

"And what if I'm not *up to* anything?" Though I know I'm only tiptoeing around the lie, it still makes my face feel still and awkward. I narrow my eyes and fight to keep looking at him.

"Then I guess you won't mind telling me what you're so excited to tell Jasper." My Dad walks past me and sits on my bed like he means for this conversation to last a long time.

Something about that, about the way he leans back and crosses his leg over his knee, makes me both nervous and brave. I bite my lip and then choose to go with brave. "Are you going to tell me why all these worried-looking strangers keep showing up to talk to you?"

His lips purse. "That's just business, Coral."

"What kind of business?" The words sail out of my mouth and, as soon as they do, I wish I could snatch them back. Curiosity has always kinda my thing, but the thick cloud settling in my chest makes me feel like that should change.

My Dad's crossed leg drops to the floor, and he leans forward. His eyes remind me of storm clouds. "Let's not forget which of us is the parent." Every word hits my ear separately, like he's throwing stones.

I look around my room, suddenly cold, and find a sweatshirt over the back of my desk chair. I put my phone on the desk and tug it on, happy not to be looking at him. When I tug my head through and push my hair out of my eyes, he's standing again. I bite my lip and wait.

"This is a time to be careful, Coral." He steps closer. "I could never forgive myself if something happened to you."

If something happened to me? My mouth falls open. "Why are we even talking about this? What's going on?"

He shakes his head, almost like he's trying to wake up. "That's what I came in here to find out. I don't like all this sneaking around you've been doing."

"I'm not sneaking around!" Well, not today, I think, and try not to let the guilt sneak in. Peeve lifts his head, ears high and alarmed, and I figure out I must have shouted. "It's okay, boy," I tell him, but he doesn't seem to buy it. With a grunt, he jumps off the bed and stands by my side.

"You and that dog," my Dad sighs.

I almost shout again, since it seems he doesn't want me to have any friends at all, but I take a deep breath instead. "He'll keep me safe," I say. "That's what you want, right?"

"I guess so." He glances around my room, then looks back at me. At least his eyes look calmer now. "I have to go to the office today. I'll be back by dinnertime."

I nod, super relieved.

"I want you to stay here, all day. Maybe you could even clean this room."

I glance around, then shrug. "They say a messy space is the sign of a brilliant mind." My Dad shakes his head. "No one I know says that."

I shrug again, wondering exactly when I got bold enough to talk back to him. And even crazier, why he doesn't even seem to notice.

He heads for the door. "I'm serious about you staying here. This is your final warning. If I find out you disobeyed me, I'm going to hire a guard to go everywhere you go. *Everywhere*."

Panic washes over me. No way I can deal with a bodyguard. "I have to walk Peeve. He can't stay inside all day."

That stops him. "That's true. I'm going to speak to Mr. Dobbins when I leave. You're to check in with him when you start the walk, and again when you come back, and you're to be gone no more than twenty minutes."

I start to protest, but then my phone chimes with a text, and Jasper's face fills my mind. "Okay, Dad," I say. "I'll let him know when I go."

He glances down at my phone, then smiles, not a real smile, but at least enough to let me know he's moving on. "Thank you, Coral. Maybe we can get a pizza or something when I get home."

"Sounds good," I tell him, itching to get to my text.

"Have a good day." He kisses the top of my head on the way out the door and, for a second, I feel small and happy, like he's Daddy again. Next to me, Peeve sniffs, and his eyes stay on my Dad until he disappears down the hall. I don't know what he sees, but I know it matters.

As soon as he's gone, I snatch my phone off the desk. Jasper's name on the face makes me smile. Finally!

Can't talk. Still feel awful. Will call when I can.

My whole body deflates. I really wanted to talk to him. I text Jasper back, telling him I hope he feels better soon, then stare down at Peeve, not sure what to do next. He blinks a few times, and his warm green eyes seem to twinkle.

"You think we should go out, don't you, boy?"

He blinks again.

Mr. Dobbin's shiny bald head pops into my mind, and my shoulders slump again. I can't do anything in twenty minutes. And then I've got it. A plan for getting in and out.

"Let's get you some breakfast, buddy," I tell Peeve. "We've got things to do today."

He licks my hand, probably because he's excited for breakfast, but also, I tell myself, because he knows we have one more friend to find, somewhere in this world, and a very small window to find her.

Chapter Eleven

I'm nervous as I walk downstairs—Mr. Dobbins is no pushover—but I just keep telling myself I can do this. I keep one hand in my pocket as I go, compass pressed into my fist, reminding me that I'm not disobeying. I'm following my *Destiny*.

As soon as we step into the lobby, I see him. I wonder if the sidewalk under his feet is worn down yet, because he always stands in exactly the same place. And then, almost like his eyes see in every direction, he turns to face me when I walk out the door of the apartment building. I whip out my biggest smile and try not to be intimidated by his wide shoulders and shiny-buttoned coat that looks more like an army general than a doorman.

"Good morning, miss," he says with a nod. "Time for big guy's walk?"

"Yes, sir." I stop, but Peeve keeps walking, clearly not recognizing Mr. Dobbins as the boss of anything. He goes far enough to yank my arm, and I start walking again. "Back in twenty," I say with a grin.

Mr. Dobbins looks at his watch and tips his hat. "I'll be here."

I gulp and nod, not sure how he can make three words sound like such a threat. Then, remembering that the clock is ticking, in lots of ways, I lead Peeve down the street a few blocks, turn the corner, let him do his giant business and collect it in my handy-dandy poop bag, then guide him back to the apartment.

"You're early," Mr. Dobbins says, eyebrows high.

I smile and shrug. "Peeve was quick today."

He nods and opens the door. "Have a good day, Miss Coral" "Thank you, Mr. Dobbins."

I walk inside and head for the elevators, trying to peek back at him without looking like I'm peeking. I make a big show out of untangling Peeve's leash, which kind of confuses him but gives me a better view of the door. And there they are, Mr. Dobbins' laser eyes. I smile and wave, then step onto the elevator.

"Phew," I say to Peeve as I push the button for the second floor. He looks up at me, like he actually knows I should have pushed the eighteenth floor, then chuffs like he just remembered the plan.

When the doors open, I hurry him out of the elevator and into the stairwell across the hall. We go back downstairs and then, instead of the door leading to the lobby, I choose the service door and hope it does what I think it does, which is lead to the back of the building. I mean, everything can't come in through the front door, right?

The hallway is dark but promising, since it looks like it runs the whole length of the building. Peeve and I walk, and he stays by my side instead of dashing ahead this time. Finally, after it starts to look like there's no way out of this hallway, I see a door marked GARBAGE.

"Thank goodness," I say, probably louder than I should have. The maintenance people could be anywhere.

I open the door, hoping we don't tumble down some giant garbage chute. Oh, my cheezy wheezy, it stinks here. The smell is like a cross between rotten eggs, urine and something so pungent, I can't even think about it! When I see beyond them, the alley. The alley!

"Woohoo!! We did it, Peeve," I tell him. He tilts his head my way, his classic 'I heard you, but I have things to do now' gesture, and I bend down and give his flank a good pat. "Thanks for playing it cool, buddy. You did great."

He snorts a little and picks up the pace.

"Good call. We have to make this fast." I match his speed and lead us to Central Park, feeling like that ticking clock is my new heartbeat.

When we get to the lake, Peeve doesn't even look for a stick, but instead stands at the shore like he's waiting for a bus. "You know the drill, don't you, boy?" I pat his head and pull out the compass.

"I wish to meet my third new friend," I say. This time, probably because I know what's coming, I feel the change in the air first. It's that heavy, building feeling that comes right before a thunderstorm, and then a shift in pressure, like the air molecules are swelling and jostling right in front of me.

I pull up the slack in Peeve's leash and tighten my grip on his collar. Though he doesn't look at me, I feel the weight of his back end against my leg. Together, we watch the water come and, as the bridge gathers itself and bends our way, I see Peeve press his body forward like he's ready to go.

I grin, thinking back to the third time I took him in the elevator. By then, he knew nothing bad was going to happen when the doors closed, and he knew he only had to put up with a few seconds of weird movement. Mostly, he knew that, when the doors opened, he got to go outside, and that made it all worth it.

The memory slips away as we're pulled back into the water bridge. It's starting to get a little old, being wet all the time, but I guess, considering where I get to go, it's not such a big deal. I do close my eyes again, since that ends up being more comfortable, and there's no way to see what's happening anyway. It only seems like they're closed for a second or two when I feel a big splash and the thud of my landing forces them open again.

Holy cannoli! Where the heck are, we this time?

All around us, giant trees stretch halfway to the sky, and I think I see mountains in the distance. I look up at them, and then down at the stream all around me. My stomach gets a little queasy. It does *not* seem like a good thing to land in the middle of a forest.

Just then a family of monkeys come near and Peeve barks loudly, three or four times, and the monkeys were long gone "It's okay, boy," I tell him. "Those monkeys were kind of cute, but I know, who knows what mischief they would have done if you hadn't scared them away." We've figured it out before and we'll do it again today."

He huffs, pretty much like he's skeptical, and I get it. I'm not feeling so great about this situation either. "C'mon, let's get out of the water." I tug him to the side of the stream, and we slog up onto the bank.

Though I really want to sit down and think about what to do next, I know that will only turn my soaking wet clothes into muddy ones. I scan the woods around me for a big rock, or maybe a tree stump, then gasp when, instead, I find a pair of eyes peering at me through the brush. I glance at Peeve, but he seems completely calm. So much for my protector.

Hoping smiles are universal, I try that first. I waggle my fingers in a little wave too, just in case that adds some friendliness. The eyes get wider, but they stay put. I guess I don't look all that friendly.

I remember that I've been able to speak the language in every place so far, so I decide to try that next. I take a deep breath and smile one more time. "Hello," I say. "It's okay, I don't mean you any harm."

Branches rustle in response, but there's no answer. I look at Peeve again, and I'm stunned to see him down on his haunches like he's relaxing in front of a fireplace or something. I could use a little help here, buddy, I think with a sigh.

"He will not eat me?" a small voice calls. A face takes shape, round and dark-eyed, and I catch a glimpse of bright pink fabric between the leaves.

"Oh, no. He definitely will not eat you. He's my friend."

A girl moves forward, dressed in something like a dress—I think it's called a saree—with that beautiful pink material draped over her shoulder like a shawl and her belly button showing just slightly above her skirt. Her sandaled feet take slow, careful steps. "You have an unusual friend," she says.

I chuckle. "That's true. And you haven't even gotten to know him yet."

She stops, looking a little scared. "I do not know if I would like that."

"Oh, it's okay. You don't have to go near him at all." I tell her, getting a little worried that the only person for miles around might run away. "Can you tell me where we are?"

"You do not know?"

"Um...no. My trip here was a little rushed."

Her eyebrows pinch together, and she looks like she might want to slip back into the trees. "This is Rishikesh."

"And what country is that?" The saree helps me think of a few, but I'm afraid to upset her by assuming anything.

"India."

"Oh, cool. I've always been interested in India. My name is Coral, and I'm from New York City."

Her mouth drops open. "You are from the USA? That is incredible."

I huff out a relieved breath. Maybe I'll at least be interesting enough to keep her talking. "What's your name?"

"Angoori."

"Oh, that's a cool name."

"Cool is good?" she says with a tiny smile. "Very good," I say with a big smile.

Angoori takes several steps forward. Just as she's close enough for me to admire the beautiful golden stitching on her saree, Peeve decides to sit up and yawn, which makes her gasp and back up almost as far as she'd come. "He has big teeth," she whispers.

I clasp my hands in front of my chest. "I promise he won't hurt you. In fact, he's really good at watching over people. Well, me really, but also my friends."

"Am I to be your friend?"

"I sure hope so! In fact, I was kind of expecting to meet you here."

The eyebrows dart together again. "I don't understand."

Uh-oh. "It's a long story, but I will explain." I glance around us, really eager for a place to sit down and talk. "Do you live around here?"

"Not far, but I do not think we should go there. Your friend might make my family nervous. And your presence would be very hard to explain."

I nod. "Good point. Is there somewhere nearby where we can sit and talk?"

Angoori waves me forward. "Follow me. There is a fallen tree this way."

"Oh, excellent. Good thinking."

She smiles and heads back the way she came. As we walk, I feel more and more grateful that she's dressed in such a bright color. It makes her really easy to follow.

After a few minutes, we reach the fallen tree. Angoori sits down, then gestures for me to join her, her eyes on Peeve the whole time.

"Down, boy," I tell him before we get too close to Angoori. As if he understands, he settles down onto his haunches, puts his head down, and looks like he might go to sleep.

"He listens well." Her hands are clasped tightly in her lap, but she seems a little less nervous.

"He really is a good boy, more like a teddy bear most of the time."

Angoori smiles. "So, what is this story you have for me?"

"Well, before starting, is it okay with you if I ask you a couple of questions? She nods in agreement. First, am I right in thinking you are thirteen years old?"

She blinks, and her eyes narrow a little. "Yes, you are correct." "And have you received some sort of surprise lately, a little gift you weren't expecting?"

Her body stiffens, and she sits up a little straighter. "How could you know that?"

"I will explain, I promise. Let me just ask a couple more questions. Are there problems with water in India? Like getting clean water, maybe? Illnesses?"

Angoori's face falls and she nods. "All of these things happen here. There are so many people in my country, and many of those are poor." She pauses, and her expression shifts for a moment. "It is my honor to be able to help in some small way."

Ah, here we go. She's definitely one of us. "You help with the water situation?"

"In my own way, yes." Her hands open and close in her lap like they have a plan of their own.

I realize it's not really fair for me to ask question after question without telling her something in return. "Okay, my turn," I begin, "but I have to warn you, this story will not be easy to believe."

She smiles. "Thank you for the warning."

"It's only fair," I tell her, and then I go back to the beginning, telling her about my wish, my gift, everything Miriam told me, the strange things I've seen water do, the two friends I met in the same way I'm meeting her, and the common problems I'm seeing in Africa, Laos, India, and New York City.

"Wait," she says. "You arrived here in a bridge made of water?"

I hang my head, knowing how crazy it sounds. "Yes. I don't expect you to believe that part yet, but when I leave here, you'll see what I mean."

She watches me, a little smile on her face. "You are correct about this being an unusual story."

"Believe me, I know."

"So, what are we to do now?"

I sigh. "You'd think I'd know that, wouldn't you, since I'm known as the Pathfinder? I guess I'm just figuring it out as I go." But Phonepasit in Laos has a special gift of communication and she has an idea about how we can keep in contact, and I've got a way we can all meet too. According to Miriam, we're all going to change the world as Ecomasters, I haven't figured that out yet."

Angoori gives a sad little laugh. "That seems impossible to believe. What can four young girls do for the entire world?"

A shiver runs through my body, more like I'm excited than scared, which doesn't quite make sense. "I know what you mean, though it seems like we all have special abilities like things we're good at. Maybe that's the key. What is it you're doing here to help with the water problem?"

She lowers her head and her gaze drops to the ground. "Now it is my turn to tell you an unbelievable story."

"I promise I'll believe you," I tell her quietly.

Angoori nods and looks up at me. "I can create and extinguish fire with my hands," she says. "I have been able to do this since I was ten."

I feel my eyes stretch wide, and I try to chill so I don't freak her out. "That's amazing," I say. "You literally can create or put the fire out by touching it?"

"Yes."

I grin. "That's a huge help in a country with water problems. You're like a superhero!" Her grin pops out too. "Perhaps I should get a cape, yes?"

"For sure!" I glance over at Peeve, and I'm relieved to see he looks totally passed out. I want Angoori to stay relaxed. "So, now that you know about my compass, can you tell me what gift you received?"

"Oh, yes," she says, leaning forward. "It's the most beautiful bindi, deep blue like the night sky, which is most surprising."

"Okay, first, what's a bindi?"

She points to her forehead, a spot right between her eyes. "A round or tear-shaped jewel. Hindu women wear them here."

Images flood my mind, women I've passed by in stores or seen on the street in New York City. "Oh, that's right. I've seen those. But what makes the color so surprising?"

Angoori's face looks a little tense. "Bindis are usually red, and they are usually worn by married women, considered the guardians of the family."

"Hmmm. Why do you think yours is blue? What could that mean?"

She shrugs. "I do not know. I was to be married before my thirteenth birthday, so I ran away from my family before that day came."

I gulp. "Married? Seriously?"

Angoori nods. "Marriage is certainly expected by my age, and it is usually arranged at birth, or soon after."

"Arranged? Wow." My brain tingles, and I realize I've heard something about arranged marriages before. It all feels really different when it's happening to a real person sitting two feet from me, though. "What do you think it means that you were given a blue bindi?"

She takes a long, deep breath. "My dream is that it means I am free. And that I can help other girls to be free. Right now, with my special gift, I can make small fires to help women and girls to boil their water before drinking. This helps to free their time for other things. This makes me very happy."

Something clicks inside me, kind of like finding the right key on a giant keyring, and I reach out and put my hand over hers. "You can do that, Angoori, and you are free to be anything you want to be. I absolutely believe that, and I know you're the perfect final piece of this wish puzzle we've all been given."

I watch her, hoping I haven't scared her off again, but her smile comes back. "Thank you, Coral. I know you speak the truth, even before you show me what the water can do."

"Oh, thank goodness! I was a little worried this would all seem too crazy." "Remember, you're speaking to a girl who can make fire appear and disappear." My mouth falls open. "You can create fire too? Holy moly, you are a superhero!"

This time, Angoori lets out a big belly laugh, and the sound is like party music to my ears. Peeve sits up at the sound, and Angoori stiffens as he moves. Afraid to lose any of the ground we've gained, I decide it's time my giant dog and I catch a wave home. Next time I'm here, I decide, I might have to leave Peeve at home.

"So, are you ready to see what I can do?" I ask, pushing my numb rear end off the bumpy tree.

"Yes, please," she says.

I walk over and grab Peeve by the collar. "Okay, I've got him. If you could lead us back to the stream, I'll show you my water trick."

Angoori nods and takes us back through the woods. Once we're at the stream, I take the compass from my pocket and hold it out to her.

"That is very pretty," she says. "What do the symbols mean? What is that language?"

I shrug. "No idea. I know it has something to do with water and the needle only moves when I make a wish." I shake it to show her, then pull

Peeve into the stream with me and wrap my fingers around the compass face. "I wish to go back to Central Park," I say and flash her a smile.

The warmth starts immediately. I almost want to let Angoori touch it, but I'm afraid to do anything to mess up the magic. I stand there, watching her face and feeling the waves that should not exist in a stream start to crash against my ankles. She stares, and her face stretches into one long 'O' of amazement.

"Goodbye," I yell, just as a small water tornado spins up my legs like a stack of hula hoops. I slam my eyes and mouth shut before it reaches my face and then, in a fraction of an instant, I'm bobbing in the lake, Central Park stretching all around me. Peeve snorts next to me, and I realize he's standing, so I put my feet down and do the same.

"Mission accomplished, boy," I say. "We did it. We found them all." A nervous flutter rattles my rib cage, reminding me that things might get really crazy from here. It can't all be magic and water rides, can it?

He snorts again and races for the grass, tail wagging like it might come loose. I follow him, trying to match his leaping strides. What a day!

I guess I really am the Pathfinder. No denying it now. Though who would deny something this cool? Not this girl, that's for sure.

Chapter Twelve

Peeve and I make our way back home, since it's almost four and I want to be exactly where I'm supposed to be when my Dad gets home. Now that I've found all three girls, and I at least have some idea of how the compass works, managing my Dad's rules and his temper seems like the hardest part of this whole thing.

And of course, after finding our way back to our secret entrance near the stinky dumpster, the door we used earlier is locked. Locked. Crumbs, now what?!

"C'mon, Peeve," I say, and tug him around the corner toward to explore. "There has to be another way in."

We walk the whole back of the building and, just as I start to get a little panicky, I notice a small box with a red button on the wall next to huge metal door, I think it is like a big garage door. "Do you think that opens it, boy?"

Peeve makes a noise—half-snort, half-sigh—but I have no idea what that means. "Should I push it?" He stares at me, then sits and lifts a giant paw to scratch behind his giant ear. "Okay," I say. "I'm going to do it."

Now he yawns, and I can't tell if he's saying, 'think harder' or 'could you hurry up already'? I decide it must be the second one, then walk up and press the button.

My heart crawls up my throat as I wait. But nothing happens. The door doesn't budge one bit.

"Come *on*," I grumble and smack the button again. Not a single noise. No movement. Nothing.

"Crap. Now what?"

Peeve whines, just a little, like he wants me to notice something I'm missing. I go over and scratch his head, then grab his leash so we can try something else. His ears perk up, and I stop and listen too.

A low grinding noise comes from the building, and then the door inches up like a grumbly old man. My heart stops. I can't move. And then I realize I do *not* know what's on the other side of that thing.

"Over here, buddy," I whisper and tug Peeve behind a wall of recycling bins and at least three long rows of 5-gallon water bottles, shoved up against the wall. He whines louder, so I stroke his ears and kiss his head as I peek out between the stacks.

When the door is all the way up, a man comes out. He looks like someone's Dad, the kind who coaches soccer and really likes baseball caps, and he's dressed in a brown maintenance uniform, so I know he works in our building.

"Really?" he says, looking up and down the alley. "We're in the middle of a heatwave and water shortage and this is not funny!" he yells. "Some of us have work to do."

Peeve sits up straighter, like he needs to protect me from this man, but I keep kissing his head. "Hang tight, boy," I tell him.

The guy disappears into the building, and the old man door starts groaning again, though this time, it sounds like music to my ears. I can definitely beat that thing, I think, and, after I count to ten, grab Peeve's leash and take off running. I'm about ready to choke on my heart at this point, but I just keep taking deep breaths and hoping for the best.

We slip inside—I have to duck, but Peeve strolls right through—and the man is nowhere in sight. "Holy cannoli Peeve," I sigh. "That was close." A door slams right when I say that, and I gulp, not sure if I'm hearing someone coming or going.

"Over here, boy," I say to Peeve and start running. We're in this big maintenance room, with tools, crates, a forklift, and way too many doors lining the walls. I have no idea which one to choose, but I decide I better pick one before that coming-or-going person finds me.

The one I pick leads me to a hallway. After that, there's just one door to pick, which makes me nervous, but what am I going to do? With a deep, fluttery breath, I swing that open...and then I grin. The stairs, thank goodness!

We don't need to mention the eighteen flights of stairs that we have to climb, but, since Peeve can take the stairs two at a time, it's a lot less work for him.

We get to the apartment, and I want to cheer as I pull out my key, but I wait. Because my Dad could be standing on the other side, eyebrows low and angry. I open the door slowly, trying to make as little noise as possible, as if that will matter. Peeve pushes in ahead of me, not one little bit quiet, and I hold my breath and listen.

Nothing. The best kind of nothing.

I scan the foyer table, the place my Dad always leaves his keys, but it's empty. He's not here.

"Wow, boy," I say, more like I'm exhaling than speaking. "That was way too close."

Peeve chuffs hard, almost like he's telling me not to do that again. "I'll try," I tell him. "That's all I can do."

I spend a few minutes taking off Peeve's leash, getting him some water, and washing my sweaty face. Literally three seconds after I re-hang my towel, I hear my Dad's key in the lock. My stomach flip-flops, telling me everything I'm trying not to know about this—I took a big risk, I *almost* got caught, I'm carrying around a lot of secrets for a middle-school kid.

"Hey there," my Dad calls, flinging his keys onto the table with a metallic crash. "I come bearing pizza."

Plastering a smile over my nerves, I go to meet him. "Smells good, Dad. Thanks."

His smile is big and real. "Thank you, Coral. I really appreciate you doing what I asked." He sets the pizza on the table and hugs me. "It means a lot."

"No problem," I tell him, feeling tiny and sad in his arms.

"Let's go eat. I'm starving."

"Okay," I say and pick up the pizza box. It smells great, but I have a feeling I'll have trouble getting it down. Turns out this saving the world stuff is very complicated.

Chapter Thirteen

Jasper's the first thing on my mind when I wake up in the morning. He *has* to be feeling better by now, and if I don't get to tell him what I've been up to soon, I'm pretty sure my head might explode. It's all just too crazy. And, even though I was in India just yesterday, it's all starting to feel like some impossible dream.

I text him to see how he's doing, then get in the shower, hoping we'll be able to talk by the time I finish. Maybe, since my Dad's currently okay with me, I can even convince him to let me go hang out with Jasper for a while. When I get back to my room, though, head wrapped in a towel, I hear my phone chime, the sound that means I have a voicemail.

"Hi, Coral. This is Sonya. I saw your text to Jasper, and I thought I better let you know it might be a while before he can call you back. He got really sick yesterday, and he's in the intensive care unit at Lenox Hill Hospital. I'll text you when he's better, okay?"

My body goes cold, and I take the towel off my head and listen to the message again, thinking I maybe didn't hear her right. But it's all the same. His sister Sonya, check. Can't call me back, check. ICU at Lenox Hill, check.

I plop down on my bed, mouth dry and head buzzing. That can't be right. Jasper's the healthiest kid I know. He doesn't even like junk food that much; I'm always the one who makes him eat potato chips with me, so I don't eat the whole bag.

And the ICU. She said ICU. That's serious. That's bad.

I glance at Peeve, who's laying on my bed and already watching me like I need guidance. "I have to get out of here, boy," I tell him. "Do I tell Dad the truth, or do I pick somewhere he won't care about, like the library?"

He puts his chin on his paws like he's thinking, and then I swear he winks.

"The library it is. Thanks, buddy." I bend down and kiss his head. Nobody looks out for me like Peeve.

Plan in place, I get dressed, grab a protein bar and a water, and text my Dad as I walk out of the apartment. I'm not going to give him the chance to say no. I tell him I have to check out my summer reading books, that I forgot about them and just remembered the book reports have to be emailed before school starts. Then I turn my ringer off, so I don't have to hear the angry chiming if he doesn't like my plan.

Head high, I hurry out of the elevator and past Mr. Dobbins. "Heading to the library for summer reading books. My Dad knows," I tell his questioning eyebrows and then keep walking like I have zero to hide.

"First I'm hearing about it," he calls.

"He probably forgot," I yell back and then hurry down the sidewalk before he can say anything else.

A few blocks later, I head down the stairs to the subway. I've never taken it alone before, but I swallow all my nerves and decide it's time. This is for Jasper.

I stop and study the map, hoping the hospital will be on it, but it's just a crazy maze of street numbers and different-colored train lines. I'm just about to dig out my phone to look up the address, which I totally do NOT want to do in case my Dad is text-yelling at me, when a nice-looking lady in a purple head scarf and dangly earrings steps up and asks me where I mean to go.

I tell her, and she traces the route with a careful finger, watching me to make sure I'm getting it. By the time the train pulls up, I have it memorized, which makes my nerves back off and leave me alone. I thank her, and she smiles. Then, though I know I only looked away for a second, she's gone. Like vanished.

I can't think about that, though. Jasper needs me.

The train doors open, and I get on. When I see an open seat, I grab it, then repeat the routes to myself as ride. The very last thing I need is to miss a stop.

It shocks me how fast we move and, two trains later, I'm back on the sidewalk and heading for the hospital. I spot the building and run up the steps, feeling like queen of the city. Here I come, Jasper.

Once inside, I realize this is a new world for me. I've never actually been to a hospital, and never by myself. Knees a little wobbly, I try to watch what everyone else is doing as I get in line for the metal detector.

"Anything in your pockets?" the wiry security guard asks. I nod.

He hands me a small round container. "Everything in here. Then walk through."

I gulp, feeling a little like I took a wrong turn somewhere. I put my phone and my key in the bin, and then, though my whole-body cramps at the thought of letting it out of my sight, I put the compass in too. I mean, if I try to sneak it through, they might take it away. That can't happen.

Without taking my eyes off the container, I walk through the metal detector and then wait at the end of the counter for the guard to give me back my things. He hands me my phone and keys, picks up the compass, then stops.

"This yours?"

I nod.

"Looks old."

I nod again.

He peers into its face, bushy eyebrows low. "What do these symbols mean?"

I shrug, buying time for my voice to work. "I don't know," I say. "I found it at a thrift shop and thought it was cool." The lie tastes sour on my tongue, but only a little. I guess I'm getting used to spitting them out.

The guard nods and smiles. "I'd have bought it too." He holds it out to me.

I wrap my hand around it and exhale, probably way too hard. "Can you tell me how to get to ICU?"

His smile stretches into a straight line, like he feels bad for me. "It's probably best to look at the directory over there. I don't get out of the lobby very often."

Nodding, I thank him and then go figure it out for myself. The pediatric ICU is on the fifth floor, same as the maternity ward. Something feels wrong about that, like new babies and super sick kids should be much farther apart. I keep my hand in my pocket, wrapped around the compass, and hope that, even if I'm not traveling the world, it might somehow make sure I end up in the right place.

When I get off the elevator, it feels a little like the compass has solved the problem for me, since there are brightly colored signs on the walls and matching stripes of color on the floor. It's pretty easy to tell where to go. I follow the orange path, more and more scared by the minute. Kids should not be here. Not visiting and definitely not sick.

It feels like I turn at least five corners and, on the last one, I spot Sonya up ahead. She's flopped on one of those waiting room couches that looks too small for a real house. I exhale hard again, suddenly wondering if I've been forgetting to breathe.

"Hey," I say quietly.

Sonya jumps. "Coral! How did you get here?" I shrug. "Subway."

Her eyes get really round. I guess it does seem like a big deal to a sixth grader, I think, then laugh at my bigshot self. My eyes were probably that round the whole time I was on the train.

"Where's Jasper? Can I see him?"

She frowns and shakes her head. "No one but family can go in, and no kids at all. I've been sitting out here waiting for hours."

"What's wrong with him?"

"They don't know for sure, or if they do, no one's told me. I heard my mom say something about water when we first brought him in, but that's all I know."

My neck tingles a little. Water again. I guess that's my whole life these days. I sure hope I figure out what it all means soon.

"Can I wait with you for a while? Maybe something will change."

Sonya slides over to one side of the couch. "Sure, if you want."

I sit, a little stunned that I got this far and then ran into such a big wall. There has to be a way to get in there. I'm literally scratching my head when I hear a door swing shut behind us.

"Is that Coral?" someone asks.

I glance over my shoulder, then jump to my feet. "Hi, Mrs. Rodrigues. How's Jasper?"

"How in the world did you get here?" she asks, then looks over *her* shoulder. "Your father isn't here, is he?"

My pulse jumps. That's a weird question. "No, ma'am. I came alone," I say, expecting a big smile and one of her famous hugs for my effort.

Instead, she frowns, and the creases look all wrong on her dark, apple-cheeked face. "Why did you come?" she asks.

"Ummm...because Sonya told me Jasper was here."

She glances at Sonya, eyes definitely not happy, then looks back at me and sighs. "I'm sure you mean well, Coral, but I'm afraid the trip was a waste of your time. You can't see him."

A weird kind of fear wraps itself around my heart and squeezes hard. I know I've felt it before, a really long time ago. "Is he okay?" I ask. "What's wrong with him?"

Mrs. Rodrigues' eyelids flutter a few times, and the tears she's fighting glisten on her lashes. "They're still doing tests, so we don't know for sure. He has non-stop diarrhea, his blood levels are off, and he's severely dehydrated. We think it has something to do with the water in our neighborhood, which hasn't looked or tasted right in a few weeks."

The fear squeezes harder and I gasp a little. "But they'll figure it out, right? When they get the test results?"

"That's what we're praying for."

Her sad, quiet voice makes me tremble. She's always so energetic and fun, laughing and snapping her fingers to music the rest of us can't quite hear. "Can I do anything to help?" I ask. "I could go get you guys food or coffee or something."

She blinks the last of the tears away. "They have those things here, Coral. We're fine."

I don't know what to say. It's like we're strangers. "Can you tell him I was here?"

"He's really out of it right now. I'm not sure if he hears us or not."

My stomach aches like I had rocks for lunch. Part of me wants to run, but the other part can't move. "I don't know what to do," I tell her.

She sighs, the longest, saddest sigh I've ever heard. "Go home," she says. "And maybe tell your father to think long and hard about what he's doing."

Now I'm the one blinking, mostly because I don't understand, but also because my eyes feel like nothing but water. "What is he doing?"

"His company's the one doing all the construction in our neighborhood, right?" "I don't know."

104

"Marchant Construction Group? That's him, isn't it?"

I nod, sincerely ready to puke. "The construction-site made Jasper sick?"

She shrugs. "Everyone was fine before his people showed up. But once they started digging, the water was different, and it was hard to get more than a trickle out of the faucet. And then this." She gestures at the door behind her, and I imagine Jasper somewhere in there, tubes and cords and monitors all around him.

"I'm so sorry, Mrs. Rodrigues," I whisper. "I didn't know." I stand there, really needing that hug but also feeling like I somehow don't deserve it.

Finally, a tiny bit of the smile I know so well breaks through. She opens her arms and her eyes get all weepy again. "I know that, honey," she says. "I'm just not myself right now."

I step closer and hug her with everything I have, instantly grateful that she's so tall. For a few seconds, I get to be little again.

And then we part, and it all rushes back: Jasper's sick, my Dad's doing something he shouldn't, and I'm supposed to be saving the world. Anger flares like a Fourth of July sparkler.

"I'll fix it, Mrs. Rodrigues. I promise." I squeeze her hand and wave to Sonya, then follow the colored lines back the way I came. My Dad better have some really good answers.

Chapter Fourteen

When I get back to the building, Mr. Dobbins eyes me like a puppy who just peed in the house again. I start to lower my head, and then I realize I don't care what he thinks. I have important things to do, too important to waste time feeling bad.

He opens the door and then holds up one gloved finger, clearly expecting me to stop and listen. "Thank you," I say, in my nicest tone, and then hurry past him. No one can say I was rude; I tell myself and jump into the elevator.

By the time the elevator doors open, I'm not feeling quite as brave, but then I picture Mrs. Rodrigues' face, and I remember what she said about my Dad's company, and I stand a little taller. Whatever the truth is, I need to know it.

I hear Peeve's tags jingling as I put my key in the lock. Poor boy. I wonder if my Dad took him out at all. He's waiting, tail wagging, when I swing the door open and, right behind him, stands my Dad.

His expression is exactly what I expected, and though my pounding heart doesn't seem as convinced as my head, I realize I don't want to run away this time. People are getting hurt. MY friends are getting hurt, and I deserve to know why.

"I don't see any books," he says and folds his arms across his chest. I stuff my keys back in my pocket and stare at him. "Books?"

He sighs and frowns, turning his mustache into an angry slash across his face. "Yes, books. Summer reading books? Isn't that what you said?"

Oooh. Yeah. At this point, it seems like I told that lie weeks ago. I lift my hands into the air. "You caught me," I say. "I made that up."

"You don't say?"

"I had a good a reason, though."

His face gets even scrunchier, and he shakes his head like he's disgusted with me. "There's never a good reason to lie, Coral, especially to your par—er, father."

I wince, because I know he was going to say parents, but I guess I see why he corrected himself. "Jasper's in the hospital."

He unfolds his arms and leans his shoulder against the wall. "Your friend Jasper?"

"Do we both know another Jasper?"

"I guess we don't. I'm sorry to hear that. Why didn't you just tell me?"

I stare at him for a long time, trying not to let that make me mad, but I just can't do it. "Seriously? You won't even let me go to his house."

107

"Well, the hospital is different."

"Yeah, it sure is," I say and walk past him to the kitchen. "Did you feed Peeve or take him out?"

"Peeve is your responsibility, Coral," he says as he follows me.

I turn on him, feeling like fumes might be coming off my head. "So that's a no?"

"I do not like your tone."

I shrug, then bend down to scratch between Peeve's ears.

"I think you should explain your attitude."

"I'm pretty sure I already did," I say, glaring at him. "I'd like you to explain the work your company is doing in Jasper's neighborhood."

His face falls slack for a minute, and he cocks his head like he didn't hear me right. "What does that have to do with anything?"

"Jasper's mom seems to think there's a connection."

"A connection to what?"

"To Jasper being in the ICU, Dad. They think he's sick from the water in his neighborhood."

Something happens to his face just then, kind of a mash-up of feelings that move too fast for me to read. Then he narrows his eyes and looks hard at me. "What did Jasper's mom say to you?"

"Pretty much what I just told you. She said everything was fine until Marchant Construction started tearing things up."

He exhales, long and hard. "She needs to be very careful about making accusations like that."

My head feels like a marshmallow on a roasting stick. "She wasn't making an accusation, she was talking to *me*, telling me what she thinks happened to her son. My *friend*." Tears fill my eyes, and I wonder if they'll turn to steam when they hit my skin. I don't know if I've ever been this angry.

My Dad seems to gather himself, and he stands a little straighter. "It's terrible that Jasper's so ill, but it has absolutely nothing to do with me or my company. In fact, it sounds like she's been listening to those eco-terrorists who've been making my life hell lately."

108

"Eco-terrorists?"

"Yes. These environmental zealots are complicating things at every turn, trying to make my efforts to help people in this city, and everywhere else, look suspicious."

"Why would they do that?"

"Because they're single-minded and clueless, unable to see past their own ineffective, tree-hugging agenda."

Though I understand the words he's using, I suddenly feel like my Dad is speaking a different language. I think back to when I was little, to how proud I used to be that my Daddy built things people needed homes and offices and schools and banks. Like magic, he made buildings out of empty space. But now, an eerie feeling washes over me, like a huge world sits behind the one I've been looking at my whole life.

"Are you doing something to hurt people, Dad?"

He blinks, over and over, like he can't believe what he's hearing. His face does that shifty thing again, and then he folds his arms across his stomach. "Do you really believe I could do that?"

"I don't know what to believe," I tell him, hating the weak, shaky sound of my voice. "That's why I'm asking."

He studies me, looks down at Peeve, then back at me. "I'm trying to help people, not hurt them, Bug. That's what I've always done."

Bug. He hasn't called me that in ages. It makes me want to hug him, and then, for just a second, makes me wonder why he'd call me that now. Why today?

All I can do is nod. I want to believe him, but a weird pressure behind my eyes makes me feel like I can't trust anything I see right now. I look at him. I realize he believes himself. Too much has happened in the past several days.

"Okay, Dad," I tell him, suddenly certain that making things okay is going to be up to me now.

Chapter Fifteen

The next morning, though my heart hurts, I know it's only going to hurt more if I sit around and think about it alone. I can't do anything about Jasper right now, and I have no idea *what* to do about my Dad, but there is something I can manage. Today, I decide, I am going to find a way to communicate with Hope, Phonepasit and Angoori. Each of the other girls I've been led to are actively helping their communities – using their gifts – and now, it's time to join together and to use mine to help who and what I can: Jasper and the city around me.

Feeling a renewed surge of energy, I smile at Peeve, feeling older than I did yesterday. And more determined. "Boy, today you're going to have to stay here and hold down the fort." I tell him, leaning down and giving him a big hug. He huffs, obviously miffed, but licks my hand once as if to say he understands. I head for the door.

Not gonna lie, it's a huge relief not to worry about my Dad this morning. My guess is that he felt bad enough about our conversation to let things rest. At least, that's what I'm assuming since I heard him leave pretty early and his briefcase is gone. The briefcase never leaves the house unless he's going to his office.

When I get on the elevator, I decide to use the secret Dumpster exit instead of dealing with Mr. Dobbins. Who knows what my Dad told him when he left? If I can at least get out and do what I need to do, I'll worry about how to get back into the building later.

The building is a bit of a ghost town today, and I don't see a single person on the stairs, in the halls, or outside the building, which is eerie. For the moment though, it clears our way for sure. I'm relieved too, though worried, I think as I hurry through the back alley. No time to dwell on that now.

Once I hit the street, I break into a quick stride. Heck, I'm nearly running. Faster is better, especially when Jasper is in the hospital, and my city is in peril.

I get to the lake, sit down, and try to wrap my head around my plan for the day. No big deal, just going to wish myself to Laos, then Africa, and to India. Then I remember the words that Phonepasit whispered in my ear, and just knew that the two of us together will be able to connect all of our new friends, even on 3 different continents! Then, when we get back, I'm going to stand here and play it cool while our new friends practice their wishing. Phew. No biggie at all. I take a big breath in and let it out.

"Ready, boy?" I say to Peeve, then realize the question is probably for me. He chuffs, and I imitate him with a grin. "Okay, let's go."

I hold out the compass. "I wish to find my friend Phonepasit in Laos."

To my relief, everything happens just like it's supposed to: warm compass, jumping needle, rolling water, and then I'm there, standing smack dab in the middle of the fountain again, surrounded by people gawking. I smile; by now I'm used to it.

I walk out, still soaking, intent on finding Phonepasit as quickly as possible. I circle back through my mind, walking through the streets and noting the landmarks I remember in my mind: right at the big Buddha shrine, left at the motorcycle shop, left again at a local restaurant with the smiling grandmother.

A familiar blue door emerges from a familiar concrete wall. Finally, I arrive at Phonepasit's house. I knock lightly as first, then harder, and finally Phonepasit opens the door. Her face widens into a bright smile – and we hug.

"I can't stay long," I tell her, "but I remember the word that you whispered into my ear about sound and water and need your help." I take out the compass.

"I need your communication gift today my friend – it's time for all of us to come together. I bring her up to date about meeting our fourth friend in India, Angoori – and according to Miriam that makes us Ecomasters, whatever that means. Now, it's time for me to help my city and to help my best friend Jasper – I don't quite know how yet…but I do know you're the right person to help. Will you assist me?"

Phonepasit blinks, then breaks into an uneasy smile.

"Of course, Coral…I'll do my best"

"We need a way to communicate. All four of us – and we're on 4 different continents. I think the key is this compass. That it will somehow unite us."

Angoori seems deep in thought.

"Coral, would you please put your hands on this with me?" Phonepasit looks at me shyly, but her voice is firm.

The compass turns blue and starts to vibrate. I smile back, feeling my heart expand. After the sadness of the past few days, a glimmer of hope opens in my heart and expands in my chest.

And with that, streams of water appear – this time, it's as if they are coming from inside of me, as if I have merged with water itself. We are surrounded by an orb of water, though Phonepasit and I can see each other clearly, like we are inside of an actual giant drop of water!

"I have an idea. Coral, please tap into the frequency of this droplet – it is a droplet that represents the water that is within our very bodies. I sense the key is this. All of us will be able to communicate telepathically – to transmit our thoughts to each other no matter where we are – and so I ask you to join me in this orb of water to create a frequency that you can gift to our other friends on our same mission."

I'm surprised, and don't fully understand the frequency part, but 100% in. Internally, I thank my lucky stars for sending me such amazing friends. Phonepasit closes her eyes. I do too.

At her outbreath, the water around us starts to sing with voices – voices, laughing, singing, as if we were inside an echo chamber, whirling, the voices of all peoples from all times, and turns crystalline. The sounds become less and less recognizable until all we can hear is a high-pitched frequency.

Phonepasit breathes deeply and says: "Done." In a millisecond, so quickly I don't even have time to blink, the giant orb shrinks to the size of the compass head, looking like a holographic droplet of water.

"Have Hope and Angoori place their hands on this compass, and they will become one with this drop. Repeat the words, "Water is what unites us – and water is how we will communicate."

I nod, looking at Phonepasit. "So," I say, cracking a wide smile, "shall we try it?"

Our voices start out soft, but gain power quickly: "Water is what unites us – and water is how we will communicate." The compass turns a rosy shade, then a metallic silver, and then a gold – and a crystalline water droplet appears on the face of the compass, and dances in the hot sun. A moment later, the water drop disperses, and travels into our hands – and our hands look nearly see-through, as if they have turned into ether, or water, or both. Woosh! As suddenly as it began, the process is complete.

"Wow. Now THAT was cool," I think.

"Yeah it was." I grin, looking at Phonepasit, realizing that I had just heard Phonepasit, yet her lips hadn't moved.

We look at each other and burst into giggles. thank water 1000X over for its gift, and I look over to see Phonepasit closing her eyes in gratitude.

"As much as I'd love to stay, I've gotta hit the road…err…water," I think, looking at Phonepasit.

"I understand, Coral! Go – we will connect again soon enough."

"Yes, we will. And I'll formally introduce you to my other friends – so we can all communicate with each other."

"Anytime you want to contact me Coral, simply repeat: "Water is what unites us – and water is how we will communicate." Then picture me in your mind's eye, and 'transmit' your thoughts my way. You can instruct the others to do the same."

I nod, satisfied, and look to a fountain inside of Phonepasit's courtyard, filled with greenery and moss and water that looks more like a mud puddle than anything else. That'll do.

"I wish to see Angoori," I announce to the compass.

The fountain churns and splashes, and I hurry to shut my eyes and clamp my mouth shut before the muddy water gets head high. For a second or two, it feels I'm caught in a washing machine or a wave pool but, as soon as I have that thought, the water stops, and we tumble into what looks and feels like a swamp. The water isn't deep, but it's everywhere, and plants grow all around me.

I open my eyes to see that I'm in the very same stream as last time. Instead of hiding in the bushes like last time, Angoori kneels at its bank, washing what looks like turquoise bed sheets.

"Coral!" she squeals and tosses the fabric aside.

114

I struggle to my feet. "Hello, Angoori. It's so good to see you again."

"For me as well. What a surprise!"

"Well, I told you I would find a way for us to stay in touch," I tell her and take the compass out of my backpack.

"Alright," I say: "Put your hands on the compass, please."

Angoori places her hands on the compass, touching mine. We smile at each other.

"I'm going to show, versus tell, so bear with me Angoori. Please repeat these words: "Water is what unites us – and water is how we will communicate."

She nods. "Okay, let's go…on the count of three. One, two, and…"

"Water is what unites us – and water is how we will communicate."

Our voices unite surprisingly strongly, and as before, a small droplet appears on the face of compass, whirling and reflecting back a crystalline frequency that is nearly audible – and then, as before, poof! The droplet travels down both of our hands, turning them transparent, and then evaporating down the rest of our body so quickly my eyes can't follow.

"Coral…that was…so COOL!" Angoori breaks out into a giant smile. Her lips don't move. I grin right back.

"Totally, Angoori. SO COOL!"

"I'm happy we'll be able to talk," I transmit to her. "It makes the world smaller."

Angoori laughs and nods. "That is exactly right, Coral. You are closer to me now. It's like you are in my heart as much as in my mind."

"Anytime you want to contact me, simply repeat: "Water is what unites us – and water is how we will communicate." Then picture me in your mind's eye, and 'transmit' your thoughts my way."

I smile at her. "I'm going to contact you this way, so you and can meet Hope and Phonepasit too."

"If I contact you this way, can you practice wishing with the bindi? I want to see if it works like my compass. And if you can travel that way, too."

She keeps nodding, clearly thrilled.

"It's time for me to go and contact Hope," I think, looking at Angoori. She nods again.

"I will…contact you soon," I say. Angoori smiles and nods.

I put my hands on the compass. I say out loud "I wish to see Hope" and picture her in my mind's eye.

The lake opens and whirls, a water stream scooping me up without much fuss (is it just me, or is this getting easier? Easier is good, considering how many times I have to travel this way) and before I know it, I'm right on my bum in the middle of a field of cracked earth.

Hope's familiar voice rings in my ears: "Coral, you never fail to make an entrance."

I laugh. We embrace, and I take out my compass. "I'm afraid my visit will be short this time – I've come to connect you with me and 2 others like us that I've met. They have abilities too– and a deep connection to water and their communities. It's a long story, but I've met two other amazing girls, Angoori and Phonepasit, from India and Laos. I know our destinies are tied together – and so I've come up with a way for us to stay in touch no matter how far away we are. I have a plan to help my community just like you're helping yours.

Part of me is in awe – how do I know how to do this? You just know, a small voice answers from within.

Hope raises an eyebrow, and then smiles. "Alright Coral – you know how much I love my community and planet. I can understand you wanting to help your community too. Let's get to it."

I grin. "Okay Hope, please place your hands on this compass and repeat with me on the count of 3: "Water is what unites us – and water is how we will communicate."

"One…two."

"Water is what unites us – and water is how we will communicate."

Once again, the water drop appears above the compass and our hands, whirling and swirling for a moment, before becoming one with our hands and then our body in a whoosh!

"Beautiful…" Hope thinks, and I affirm. "It's like water is joining us and joining *with us.*" Hope's mouth opens, realizing neither of us have opened our mouths.

"Amazing, right?" I grin.

"Beyond…" transmits Hope.

Anytime you want to contact me, simply repeat: "Water is what unites us – and water is how we will communicate." Then picture me in your mind's eye, and 'transmit' your thoughts my way.

Satisfied, I hug her, and then go back to the middle of the stream and wish us to the lake. When we arrive, I climb out of the water, sit down on the bank, and then lean down and kiss the grass. That could have gone so wrong, but here we are, just like it was all supposed to go this way.

I sit down, rest, and have a snack, and catch my breath. Knowing that time is of the essence, I don't wait long before I make my first transmission. Hope answers with a chirpy, "HI!", which makes me chuckle a little. I tell her to wait two minutes, then wrap her hand around her pendant and wish to see me. I contact Phonepasit and then Angoori, giving them both the same instructions with their unique gifts to wish their way to me here in the city.

Just as I'm done with Angoori, I hear a low rumbling. Seconds later, the water rises, looking like a stubby waterspout. Before I can even blink, Hope rolls out of the water and lands at my feet.

She looks up at me with such a mix of shock and relief that I can't help giggling. "Weird, huh?" I say.

"*So* strange." She grins and rises to her feet, then turns her head in every possible direction. Her eyes get rounder by the second. "But it worked. I'm here. I cannot believe I am standing in the middle of New York City and you are correct my dear, it is much hotter here than in my village."

"Yep, this is it, and—"

The water churns all over again, Hope and I peer together at water's edge. We are shocked out of our amazement by Phonepasit, scooting back to get out of her way STAT as she glides onto shore towards us on a giant wave.

Hope's mouth falls all the way to her chest. "Who is that?"

I run to Phonepasit and help her to her feet. "I'll do introductions in a minute," I tell them both. "We should have one more in just a sec."

When the water swells this time, it rushes at us sounding like a fully heated teakettle. The sound makes me nervous at first, but then I realize I'm hearing Angoori shriek as she rides the wave. She rolls across the grass, sari twisting and fluttering around her. When she stops, she looks up at me with the widest eyes I've ever seen.

"That was unbelievable," she cries.

We all burst out laughing. As we gather in a circle, I look at my new friends and take a minute a minute to soak in the image of the four of us, magically gathered from all across the world. Though I still don't know how it's all possible, I do know that I'm already a different person, and we've barely gotten started.

"So... here we are," I say, smiling at each of the. "May I present Hope from Malawi, Phonepasit from Laos, and Angoori from India."

They nod and smile to each other, all managing to look both thrilled and shell-shocked. For a second, a flash of worry washes over me. I know I can speak to each of them, but can they speak to each other? That could make things really complicated.

"Alright everyone," I say, taking out my compass. Now I want to make sure we can all speak to each other. Let's all put our hands on the compass and say together, ""Water is what unites us – and water is how we will communicate."

All 4 of us gather around the compass and place our hands on each other in a happy pile.

"Alright, crew," I say, smiling. "On the count of three. One, two…"

"Water is what unites us – and water is how we will communicate."

Once again, the drop of water appears above our hands on the face of the compass, vibrating at a near crystalline speed, then pop! Traveling down all of our hands, turning them clear, right before the now familiar whoosh! The drop flashes down our bodies, integrating into our forms once again.

"That never gets old," I think, smiling.

"Miracles never do," transmits Angoori, and I hear her distinct 'voice' sounding through my mind.

"Angoori? Could you please tell us something about yourself? I want to make sure we can all understand."

She nods. "I am more than a little scared of water," she shares without moving her lips, topped off with a sheepish grin.

I chuckle, because that's just funny and, before I can check in with the others, Hope and Phonepasit burst out laughing.

"That is unfortunate, my new friend," Hope transmits. "I have a feeling we will be eternally damp in the days to come."

"We will be with you." Phonepasit reaches out and squeezes Angoori's hand. The way her face shines makes my already happy heart even happier.

"This is most wonderful," Angoori transmits. "I am guessing I won't be afraid much longer."

Phew. We can all talk to each other. Thank you, compass.

"Okay, friends," I tell them. "I don't want any of you to get into trouble at home by staying too long. There will be other trips to New York City, I'm sure."

The girls nod their agreement, and I send them on their way.

Here's hoping whatever waits for us in the water isn't more than we can handle.

Chapter Sixteen

I feel pretty good about myself the next day. Coral the Pathfinder, and Phonepasit the Communicator, carried out water drop plan perfectly. Even better, I got back home before my Dad came home from work and, gift of all possible gifts, Mr. Dobbins was not anywhere in sight when I got to the front door. That only happens like two times every day, for no longer than three minutes. I guess everyone has to pee sometime, but it hurts my head to try and calculate exactly how lucky I got. Peeve seems to be OK, but he is agitated – and I can see why, because the door to my room is closed. He's been in here all day. "What's up, boy? Let's get you outside…"

I stroll into the kitchen, only to find a complete stranger sitting at our granite island reading a newspaper. My sneakers squeak when I stop, and I just stare, not sure if I should call the police or what.

"You must be Coral," the man says. He looks a little like a police detective, with the shortest possible haircut and a dark suit.

I gulp. "Who are you?"

"You can call me Henry."

I step forward and grip the granite, hoping I don't look as nervous as I feel. "Okay, Henry. Can I ask why you're in my kitchen?"

"You don't have to worry," he says and smiles. "I work for your Dad."

"And you're working here today?"

He nods. "I guess you could say that. I'm here to keep an eye on you."

Dread creeps over me. This is not good, not good at all. I try to stand tall and act cool. "I don't need a babysitter."

"The word your Dad used was bodyguard."

"Did something happen that I need a bodyguard?"

Henry purses his lips and studies me. "Pretty sure it had something to do with you sneaking out yesterday."

My mouth falls open. "He said I sneaked out?"

He taps the top of his lip with one finger and stares up at the ceiling for a minute. "I think he said the doorman mentioned it."

The flush in my cheeks only makes me madder. This is not right. I shouldn't have to be prisoner in my own home. And I just don't buy that there's new danger out in the city waiting just for me. Why would anyone be after me?

"Okay, then," I tell him, needing a little time to regroup. "I guess I'll be in my room then."

"Got it," he says and goes back to his newspaper.

I stand for a moment, glaring at him. His 'friendly guy' act is super annoying. Might as well call him what he is—a prison guard!

Wanting to remind him this is still MY house; I fling the refrigerator door open and stare inside. I'm not really hungry, but I'm making a statement here. I grab some string cheese and slam the door shut, then march out of the kitchen like I have someplace to be.

Which I do. Lots of places that aren't my bedroom. I just haven't figured out where yet. And now I don't know how I'll get there.

Peeve looks up at me when I get to my room. At first, he looks a little annoyed to be pulled from his snooze, but then his brow ridge furrows. I know he can tell I'm upset.

"This Henry guy has to go, Peeve."

He yawns then cocks his head at me.

I wander around my room as I munch the string cheese, scanning my brain for some kind of a scheme. I pop the last bit of cheese in my mouth and glance down at my desk. Under a sock, I see the copper ball from Miriam's house peeking out and my pulse freezes. That's it. That's where I need to be today. Miriam's house. I need to tell her that I found everyone, and then I need to find out what happens next.

"Okay, boy. I need your help."

Right on cue, he yawns again, jumps off my bed, and walks over to sit in front of me. The sight of my best friend, always ready to help, tugs at my heart. I bend down and kiss his nose. Then I scratch under his chin in exactly the spot he loves.

"You can't come with me this time, okay, buddy?"

He raises his chin higher, not ready to be done with the scratch.

"I'm sorry to leave you, but I'll be back as soon as I can."

Peeve whimpers, really softly, then gives his head a huge, let's-get-this-show-on-the-road shake.

"Thatta boy," I tell him and kiss his nose one more time. "I love you, Peeve."

After making sure I have the compass in my pocket, we go back down the hall. When we get close to the kitchen, I tell Peeve to stay. He sits and looks very intimidating. Pleased, I walk back down the hall, but then I hear his jingling behind me and my heart sinks.

"Peeve, no," I whisper. "You have to stay."

He sits.

I turn away and the jingling starts again. "Come on, buddy. Sit and stay."

He walks up and licks my hand.

With a big huff, I lead him back, closer to the kitchen. "Now, stay," I say, as loud as I dare.

Clearly tired of this game, he barks. I cringe and wait. After a few minutes go by, I finally breathe. Then I hold up my hand, hoping he'll remember the hand sign from his puppy training. He chuffs and nods, and I think we're good. I start down the hall.

"What's up?" Henry's voice sounds casual and not, and it stops me cold.

"Um, nothing. Just doing a little training with Peeve."

"He's gotta be tough to train."

"Not really," I say, an idea taking shape in my head. "Can you do me a favor, Henry?" He smiles, but his eyes narrow. "Depends on what it is."

"Can you give Peeve a treat? They're in the pantry closet in the kitchen."

"You're too busy? Aren't treats part of the training?"

I grin, though I'm super annoyed. This guy is good. "They totally are," I tell him. "I just forgot to grab them, and I really have to...um... you know." I tilt my head toward the hall. Then I cross my legs for effect.

"Oh, uh, yeah. Sure. Come on, boy." He waves at Peeve, but Peeve stays put.

"Go on, Peeve," I say, trying to give him the eye.

Peeve stares at me, makes me think hard about what I'm about to do. Finally, after seconds that feel like hours, he turns and follows Henry.

"Thank you, buddy," I whisper and dash into the bathroom. I don't lock the door, since I'm going to have to leave the shower running. That only seems fair to poor Henry. I put my ear to the door and, when I don't hear any talking or jingling outside, I turn on the shower, wrap my hand around the compass, and step into the spray.

"I wish to see Miriam," I say, then squeeze my eyes shut. By now, it's totally automatic.

A weird sucking feeling winds its way through my body, making me feel long and thin. And then, as soon as that thought fills my mind, I hear a huge splash, and water smacks my face just as my butt hits something hard.

A scream echoes all around me, and I open my eyes to see Miriam's terrified face. She's in her robe, clearly about to enjoy the bath I've crash-landed into. I stare up at her, not sure if I should cry or laugh. Then her lip wiggles, and mine does too. We're both snorting with laughter in seconds.

"I guess this compass thing really works," I sputter, and we laugh harder. "That it does, my dear. That it does."

124

Chapter Seventeen

W rapped in a big, fluffy bath towel, with my wet clothes spinning in Miriam's dryer, I follow her into her office. There aren't as many plants in here as the rest of the house, but the number of clipboards and paperwork has to be more than double. Whatever she's studying, she sure is serious about it.

"I'm very happy to see you, even if your arrival was somewhat unconventional." She grins and gestures to a maroon wing chair next to her desk. "And it seems fair to assume you've had success with the compass?"

I laugh, and the sound bounces back to me in the small room. "I think so, though I still don't quite know where I'm going to end up a lot of time. And I always look like I just got caught in the rain."

Her eyes twinkle. "So, yes. Definite success." She leans back, her office chair tilting away from me. "Tell me where you've been. Who you've met?"

I exhale, warm relief seeping across my body. It's so nice to just be able to talk, without having to think too hard about what I say. The names and places tumble out, along with the story of programming the water droplet, our newfound telepathic communication, and the girls' quick trip to New York City.

Miriam's smiling at me, her eyes crinkling, and tearing up, shaking her head in amazement.

"And all four of you were together in Central Park yesterday?"

"Yeah," I say carefully, suddenly worried I did something I shouldn't have. "Is that against the rules or something?"

She smiles and shakes her head. "No, my dear. In fact, all of this means that you are progressing even more quickly than I dared to hope."

I relax again, and even feel a little proud of myself. "Oh, that's good," I say and lean back in my chair too. "I was won—" My gaze lands on a piece of paper of her desk, or actually, on a symbol in the corner of that paper, and the words in my mouth dry up.

"Is something wrong, Coral?"

I point, then look at her. "What is that?"

She frowns and looks down at her desk, then back at me. "To what are you referring?"

"That," I say. "The symbol. The waterfall volcano thing."

Miriam smiles like she has a secret. "So, it is time."

"Time for what?"

"Time for you to learn more about me, about where I come from and how you are connected."

I gulp, the curious part of me thrilled, but the kid part of me a little worried about what comes next.

Miriam leans forward. "Have you seen the symbol before?" I nod. "On my Dad's computer."

"Did you ask him about it?"

"No. He kept closing the document every time I came into his office, so I figured I shouldn't."

She crosses her arms and props her chin on her fist. "That was probably smart. It might keep him off the trail a little longer."

"The trail?" I feel a little sick. This seems very complicated.

Miriam lowers her arms and reaches for my hand. Her touch makes me feel a little better. It's nice to have someone to comfort me.

"I have much to tell you, Coral, but I'm also concerned that the situation is escalating more quickly than expected. I will take some time to explain, and then I will let you decide what to do."

"You'll let *me* decide? Why me?"

"Because you are the Pathfinder. You are the reason all of this is even possible now."

I shake my head, uncomfortable with the weight of her words. Traveling around the world on water waves is one thing, but I'm not ready to be the one making decisions.

Miriam squeezes my hand. "Do not fear," she says. "All is as it is meant to be."

Great. That sounds a lot like 'there's no way out.' I take a really deep breath and look her in the eye. "So, what do you have to tell me?"

She smiles. "Excellent. Courage is always the best choice." She lets go of my hand, swivels her chair toward her desk, and picks up the piece of paper I noticed earlier. "This symbol represents a group I am part of, or, more correctly, a group that is part of me."

A sigh slips out. As much as I like this lady, it's driving me nuts that she speaks in puzzles.

Almost like she reads my thoughts, Miriam pauses and presses a hand to her lips. "I will try harder to be clear," she says after a moment.

My mouth goes dry. How did she do that?

"I am a guardian of the island of Illuminada, a magical island in the Amazon region of Brazil, accessible only by boat, and only during the dry season. At other times of the year, the island is invisible under water, is as if it does not exist. And in fact, the emblem you describe as a 'waterfall volcano' is actually a depiction of a hidden portal located within a very special tree, which is the only way to reach Illuminada."

I sit up straight and clutch the arms of my chair. This sounds way cool but also super confusing and impossible. "Okay, one thing at a time. First, what do you mean by guardian?"

"A caretaker? A defender? To be simple, the island of Illuminada is home to an ancient training ground for guardians of Mother Earth. It is the home of my people, and we exist to protect it and facilitate its power."

Okay...I guess that's clear...ish. "And what does that have to do with me? And my Dad?"

She sighs. "Those are two different issues, my dear. You are a crucial part of the work Illuminada exists to perpetuate. You are meant to go there, to learn its lessons, and, together with your new friends, become a team of EcoMasters, who will endeavor to heal the world."

The air gets heavier around me. That's a lot to take in. "And my Dad?"

"Unfortunately, your father has lost his way. He now represents the opposition. His agenda is at odds with ours."

A wave of goosebumps attacks my skin. "So, he's trying to ruin the world?" "Trying may be the wrong word, but the outcome will likely be the same." "And I'm supposed to stop him?"

She reaches for my hand again. "Not just you, Coral. You and your friends are now the first four Ecomasters of your time; you and all those who will join your efforts. You are the reason for the hidden training island of Illuminada. This is not one task, but many; not just one problem to solve, but the path to solving all. Unfortunately, that path does not stretch into infinity. If we do not restore balance to the world, we will see catastrophic change within months."

Months?? It feels a little hard to breathe again, and I tilt my head and look at her. "You remember I'm only thirteen, right?"

"I do. And that is as much a strength as a challenge." "If you say so," I murmur.

"I not only say so, I promise it is true."

My body suddenly gets twitchy and restless. I think I've done as much thinking as I can handle right now. "Okay, then. Now what?"

"Now you must make a decision." "About what?"

"That, too, is up to you."

Oh, for Pete's sake. Are Miriam and her people allergic to straight answers? I bury my face in my hands then rub my cheeks like it might get my brain chugging. Fine, I decide. Let's do this.

"You can take me to the island?" I ask.

She jumps to her feet. "Indeed, I can, dear Coral. I simply needed to know that is what you desire."

Could have just asked, I think, then tuck my annoyance away. Maybe things have to happen like this for some reason. "I guess I should contact the others and tell them to join me. How long should I tell them? Can we be there in an hour?"

Miriam grins. "We can be there much sooner than that. You wish to go now?"

I shrug. "Might as well, yes?"

"Most definitely."

I glance down and realize I'm still wrapped in a towel. "I'll just get dressed, contact the crew, and then we can go."

"Excellent." She hurries to the door. "I'll grab your clothes and meet you in the bathtub."

I can't help chuckling.

I say out loud, grasping the compass with both hands, keeping Angoori, Hope, and Phonepasit in my mind's eye: "Water is what unites us – and water is how we will communicate."

All three of them say their hellos – and blessedly, it's as if the water has its own way of sorting out the chaos, because it's like having a three-way conversation in person.

"Ok guys," I transmit. In 10 minutes, make your wishes: "I wish to be with Coral for Ecomasters training on the island of Illuminada."

I hear them think "Illuminada? Where…or what is that?" before they all agree. Weird is the new normal.

"Ok Coral – see you all in 10," says Angoori. The other two echo Angoori. We're in businesses. I look over at Miriam, who has been watching me this whole time with a mix between awe and humor.

Miriam smiles her secret smile again, then dashes out of the office. I follow her, a small girl in a big towel, ready to do whatever I have to do to get us to Illuminada.

Chapter Eighteen

After draining the bath water and turning on the shower, a smiling Miriam urges me to step into the bathtub with her. "Your move, Coral," she says. "Take my hand and make your wish."

I nod, trying not to think about all the things I don't want to think about: how much angrier my Dad is going to get, how much sicker Jasper could get, how strong and smart I'm going to have to be to do this right.

"All will be well, I promise," Miriam whispers.

"Okay, then." Grasping the compass tight, I take a deep breath and close my eyes. "I wish to be on the island of Illuminada to learn how my new friends and I can save our Planet."

The feeling is similar this time, that same stretching and thinning, though also a weird, jittery pulse. I wonder if that's my heartbeat. Or maybe Miriam's? Are we both that nervous?

And then the wondering is over; my feet are on the ground and I open my eyes to the sight of golden tea-colored water sloshing around my ankles.

My first thought is to wonder if, when we traveled across the world, we also somehow traveled through time. Everything about this place seems ancient and timeless, from the gigantic, sweeping trees—arms stretching up to shield the earth and also bending low like they mean to hug it—to the massive, snaking roots bending in every direction as they slip down and out of sight, and the glittering shafts of sun piercing the branches.

In the center of the shocking beauty, one gargantuan tree towers overall, almost like it holds up the sky. My eyes widen as I realize that the earth—*the earth I'm currently standing on*—circles, but doesn't touch, the tree's trunk. It's like this 'sky tree' is planted somewhere far, far below, which makes me wonder what the heck we're standing on.

"Holy, holy cannoli," I whisper.

Still holding my hand, Miriam gives it a squeeze. "I knew you'd love it," she says.

Together, we step out of the little stream at our feet and stand on its bank. I check my phone, wondering how much time has passed since I called the others. Somehow, it's already been thirty minutes, and I worry a little that my friends made their wishes before I actually landed here. What if they're wandering around in whatever lies between here and New York City? They can always reach me telepathically if need be.

I turn to Miriam, afraid to ask and afraid not to ask, then hear a strange pop-splash behind us. I glance back and can't help but grin at Phonepasit's face. She looks stunned and terrified, but also relieved. She steps out of the stream just as two more pop-splashes echo like breaking balloons. "Eeek," she screams and runs my way.

"You are safe here," Miriam says and puts a hand on her shoulder, which immediately calms her.

Phonepasit blushes. "I am not used to this sort of thing." "Nor I," Hope says, slogging out of the stream. "But it's fun."

Angoori smiles and says nothing, then steps onto the bank and wrings out the bottom of her sari.

Miriam faces the group and beams at us. "Coral, would you introduce your friends?"

"Umm...sure. This is Phonepasit from Laos, Angoori from India, and Hope from Malawi. And this is Miriam, a friend of my mother's and a guardian of this place."

"And what is this place?" Hope's voice is strong but careful.

"Perhaps we should be the ones to explain."

My mouth falls open as a group of people steps out from what looks like a dark, gooey slash in the sky tree. How is that possible? Where in the world—*literally*—did they come from?

In a flash, Miriam runs toward them, hugging and laughing. She turns back to us. "It's my turn for introductions. These are my fellow guardians of Illuminada, Saulo, Etienne, and Cara."

The three nod in turn, their eyes friendly but their stiff, straight bodies still in warrior mode. I nod back, afraid to do anything else, but then Miriam waves us forward excitedly. After more greeting and hugging, we all stand back and look at each other. The suspense makes me nervous. "So, now what?" I can't help asking.

The guardians smile but say nothing.

Hope nudges me. "What are we to do, Coral?"

I shrug, not wanting to admit I have no idea. I wrack my brain for a clue, something Miriam said before we left her home. "Lessons," I blurt. "We're here to learn lessons to learn our Ecomaster-y stuff, things this place can teach us. Isn't that what you said, Miriam?"

Miriam beams and turns to her friends. "You see, I told you she is worthy. She understands even before she understands."

They all nod and smile at me like I just turned straw into gold or something. I shrug and look away. I wish we could just get to the point.

Like she knows what I'm thinking, the guardian named Cara, a tiny, raven-haired woman with deep blue eyes, raises her arms in the air. "Just as the earth is our home, the island of Iluminada is our school," she says, peering up into the trees. "Everything here, and elsewhere, is connected and dependent upon everything else. And, at the heart of that connection, is the earth's lifeblood: water."

It feels like I get taller as she speaks, almost like my cells are soaking up the information. Suddenly, I'm not just a girl from New York City, trying to understand what's going on in her city and in her family, but I'm something else. A warrior. A protector. An Ecomasters *guardian-in-training*.

Once again, just like she knows my thoughts, Cara steps closer. She walks between us— Hope, Phonepasit, Angoori, and me—placing her hands on our shoulders, and then on the tops of our heads.

"I can feel the good in each of you, the honor in your intention and the light in your spirit. I can feel your new understanding growing, drop after drop swelling into a great pool of knowledge and power. It has been many years since we four stood in your shoes, as scared as we were eager, and it is a great gift to meet you, and to welcome you to join our quest."

I glance at Miriam and, for second, she looks my age, my size. I stare at her, mind blown, and wonder if she was the Pathfinder of her group. What if my compass used to be hers? I almost want to cry at that, at the idea of having something handed down to me, even if it doesn't come from my mother.

Next to me, Angoori seems a little agitated too. "What is happening, Coral?" she whispers.

"I think we're about to find out," I tell her and grab her hand. "It's okay. I know it's going to be okay."

134

"Yes, we can do this," Phonepasit says. "Do not worry, we are with you." She moves in next to Angoori and takes her other hand.

A smiling Hope finds my other side, and my other hand. And then, moving like water, kindness flows between us. It feels strong and solid, like family, and my face can't decide whether to smile or sniffle.

"Ah, there it is," Miriam says. "The first lesson is complete. Like the difference between one finger and a fist, we are all stronger together."

"Then let us continue." Etienne walks over, stands face to face with Hope, and studies her carefully.

After a few moments, he moves in front of me. His ebony eyes feel like magnets, and all I can do is stare back. Angoori is next, and then Phonepasit. Finally, he steps back, and the four guardians form a line in front of us.

"On behalf of Yemanya, Amazon goddess of the water, creator of the island of Illuminada, and all the ancient spirits who offer their wisdom, strength, and protection to all Ecomasters, it is our great pleasure to invite you to join our ranks," booms Saulo, whose deep voice sounds a little like a Viking horn.

Miriam nods. "The path of an Ecomaster is not easy, but it is noble and necessary. Though you have all been chosen, you must now choose."

She waits, staring at us. The back of my neck gets hot, and I look all around me, wondering if I missed some clue in the dense green scenery. It would have been nice to get some instructions before we did this thing. Or even just a hint now and then.

A few more awkward moments pass, and then I can't stand it. "What are we choosing?" I ask quietly, kind of hoping Saulo won't be the one to answer.

"To join us," Cara says with a tiny smile.

"Ooohhh. Got it." I look at my friends, and we exchange nods.

"Yes," I say. "I choose to join you."

Miriam's face shines like someone flipped a switch behind her eyes. One by one, she looks to Hope, Angoori, and Phonepasit and, one by one, they make the same choice. Tears find me as I watch, though I'm not sure why. This just feels big—heart big, life big, planet big. And I get to stand in the middle of it.

"Welcome, friends." Miriam rushes up to hug us all and then steps back and clasps her hands in front of her chest. "Now, the real adventure begins. Please follow me." Darting like a pixie toward the sky tree, she stops next to its trunk, turns back, and holds out her hand. "Coral, you will go first," she says.

"Go first?" I make myself keep walking, but I do not like the sound of that. "I don't get it."

"Oh, you will," she tells me with a little giggle.

Before I can even brace myself, she grabs my shoulders and guides me toward that dark slash in the tree. From up close, it looks like more of a hole, or a gap. Fists clenched, I peer at it, hoping I'll figure out what she wants before my face smacks the wood.

I feel her hand pressing on the top of my head, making me duck low, and then, almost like some weird, backward wind sucks me up, I'm pulled into the slash. It's dark but cozy, not gooey at all, which is a big relief.

"You might want to plug your nose," she calls from outside.

"Huh?" I start to look back at her, totally confused, but then my feet slide out from under me and my butt crashes down with splash. " Aaaaahhhhhh," I scream as I tumble backward down what feels like the biggest water slide in existence.

For a crazy number of seconds, I flop and twist and turn, falling down, down, down, so much farther than should make sense. I'm moving so fast I can't even scream anymore, and every new dip and drop makes me worry about when, and WHERE, this thing might stop.

Finally, there's a strange surge, like a water bubble swelling beneath me, and then I bounce to a stop, shocked and out of breath. A stunning green-gold waterfall whooshes in front of me, and I stare like I'm hypnotized until a wailing Angoori splash-slides into view. We gape at each other, eyes like round like quarters, as Hope and Phonepasit and Miriam tumble and skid into the damp space.

"What did you think of the portal?" Miriam asks with a chuckle.

My brain explodes. Suddenly, the symbol makes sense. Water in a tree. I get it, I get it! "That was unbelievable," I tell her as I struggle to stand.

"Help each other, girls," she calls as she leaps to her feet. "We have much to see and do."

Stunned and soaking wet, the four of us swap some nervous giggles and then chase after Miriam. The last thing we need is to lose her on the other side of the waterfall. She's right there, though, on the other side of the water, smiling and waiting for us to catch up. I start to smile back at her, and then the new world around me snags my eye.

O. M. G. Seriously.

All I can do is gasp. Breathtaking colors and textures stretch in every direction. I stare and stare, realizing I don't even have words for what I'm seeing and hearing. Giant butterflies seem to sing like angels, as beaming rays of rainbow light embrace golden waterfalls in all directions and pink—PINK! —dolphins swim joyfully in basin pools. Beneath our feet, green and golden ferns look like velvet grass.

In the distance, a field of flowers dances to a gentle breeze. In the middle of the field, I spot a gigantic boulder-like tower of diamond, so clear it's almost invisible. As I watch the way the flowers move, every face turned toward the boulder, I start to wonder if the diamond is actually making them dance.

All around us, I see trees of every imaginable shape, size, and color, like autumn in fairyland. Some are so tall I just have to imagine their domed tops. All around me, the sky glows a light violet purple prettier than any sunset I can remember. I give myself a little pinch, not completely sure this is real. How can so much color and light to exist so far below the ground?

"It's amazing, yes?" Miriam beams at us.

"I need a bigger word than amazing," I tell her, and my new friends all nod.

She grins. "Well said, Coral. Now please, girls, follow me once again. Let's get you settled for the night and, tomorrow, your training will begin."

Though I'm trembling with excitement, a small wedge forms in my gut, like something's pushing my stomach up into my ribs. My Dad is going to lose it when I don't come home tonight. And then I remember that I basically disappeared into thin air this morning. By now, he's already lost it six times over.

Anyway, it doesn't matter. What we're about to do is way more important than any of that. And I don't plan to miss out on a single second of it.

Chapter Nineteen

When I open my eyes in the morning, I see a rainbow of leaves and sky beyond a thatched roof. A wave of panic washes over me, and then I remember where I am and what I saw and did last night. That's right; it's morning in the Amazon. The frickin' Amazon. Wow, what a week it's been!

Knowing we have A LOT to learn today, I sit up and look around, then smile at the sight of my new friends spread out on hammocks all around me. They're all still sleeping hard, and I think about snuggling back into my pod, wrapping it around me. I mean, no one said we have to start when the sun comes up. But, after a night spent sleeping under what feels like newly discovered stars, the bright light of day whispers that more unimaginable things wait outside this hut.

I put on my shoes, then walk over and peek out. Miriam smiles from a stump near the campfire circle, then gestures for me to join her.

"Good morning," I say and sit down next to her.

"Did you sleep well?"

"Sure did." I grin and stretch. "I think this is the freshest air I've ever breathed in my life."

"Well, they do call this part of the world the 'lungs of the planet,'" she tells me. "Together with the oceans, they create most of the oxygen we breathe."

I look around, blown away to not only be talking about the Amazon River basin but to be sitting right in the middle of it while I do. "I guess I have a lot to learn about how the earth works."

"We all do, dear Coral. I know much, but our world is constantly changing, and so our skills must change as well."

"When do we get started today?" I ask, just as my three friends lumber out of the tent.

Miriam smiles and waves them over. "Now that everyone is awake, we will have some breakfast and then begin. Angoori, would you be kind enough to work your magic?"

Angoori grins and nods as Hope and Phonepasit find stumps around the circle. We all watch as she carefully arranges the logs and tinder. I hold my breath when the big moment comes, still amazed that I actually know someone who can throw fire from her fingertips. Face still and focused, she lets the flames fly, igniting the wood in seconds.

Before long, we're eating big bowls of tapioca with acai berries and boiled bananas. It's so good I finish mine in about five minutes and go back for seconds. "I think the air here makes me hungry," I say, realizing everyone is looking at me.

140

"Eat all you can," Cara tells me. "You will need every bit of energy you can find today."

That sounds a little intense, but I take a deep breath and decide to be excited instead. I might never again do anything this cool. Of course, as of last week, I never expected to own a magical compass and travel around the world on miraculous water waves, so who knows?

When we've all finished, we're taken to the facility's version of classroom, open on all sides with a thatched top and a circle of big logs for us to sit on. A sand box with a sharp-tipped branch sits in the middle of the circle. In the center of the sand square, someone has drawn what I'm now thinking of as the 'water tree' symbol and, unlike when I saw it on my Dad's computer or the paper in Miriam's office, it looks just right here, made *of* the sand instead of just in it.

Excitement weaves its way through my body, deeper than I've ever felt it before. I study my friends as they take their seats, hoping they feel it too, and wondering how this school room compares to what they're used to. Angoori looks the most shocked and, based on what she told me about her life, I wonder if she's even had to chance to attend school ever. I flash her my biggest smile, but the one she sends back makes mine feel tiny. This is going to be a good day, I think.

"We're going to begin by studying eco-systems," Cara tells us. "As Ecomasters, you can only do your best work if you understand how the planet functions and how these various systems work together and impact one another."

I'm listening hard, but the word Ecomasters lingers in my ear. Is that what we'll be? I have to admit, it sounds pretty heroic, and the idea makes me sit up a little straighter.

"In this place, we learn to recognize and value the power and beauty of nature, both seen and unseen, visible and invisible, silent and beseeching," Cara continues. "Here, we work to understand and emulate the lessons of the turtle, the vulture, the river dolphin, the blue butterfly, the Mangrove trees, and the very sand and stones beneath our feet.

Through their examples, we can heal our world and evolve our species, reversing the despair and destruction that currently plague our planet."

Wow. Her words land heavy on my skin, and a tiny worry tingles in my brain. I know I'm strong and smart but am I strong and smart enough for *this*?

My pocket buzzes just then, and I jump, thinking some giant bug just stung me. I slap my thigh, then realize what's going on. Before I can get the phone out of my pocket, it's buzzed like six more times.

My skin goes cold, and I'm terrified to look. I don't get a lot of texts as it is, and never six in a row. It has to be my Dad.

Coral, where are you?

How did you get away from Henry? He says you just disappeared. Did you do something to him?

Are you okay?

I can't believe you didn't come home last night.

I need you to text me back.

I don't want to have to call the police. Please don't make me do that.

Everything else melts away as I scroll through the texts. I can tell he's worried, but he also seems mad, and that bothers me. Shouldn't he just be concerned? My heart pinches a little, in a deep place I don't use very often. I try to breathe through it and put my phone away. But not before texting Jasper quickly.

"Love you Jasper. I don't know if you'll get this, or how you're feeling, but I'm going to help make this right." I breathe in deeply, and press send.

"Now that we've talked about the science of the world, let's go put some things into practice," Miriam is saying. "Becoming an EcoMaster is about movement as much as knowledge, about working with the elements as you work to protect them."

"Isn't this amazing, Coral?" Phonepasit turns to look at me, her eyes bright. "With these ideas, we can do so much good."

I nod and lean closer, hoping her excitement will seep my way. "It is awesome," I say as we follow the guardians to what looks like an obstacle course made of things found in the jungle. My mouth falls open. It's like I'm on a movie set or something.

"Over here," Saulo calls. He's holding a huge stick, kind of like Gandalf's staff but thinner. "We're going to begin stealth and self-defense instruction."

Beside me, Hope chuckles. "I would never get to learn such things back home. And I feel sorry for the bullies in my village from now on."

Her grin makes me laugh. "I have a feeling we're all going to go home feeling like completely different people," I say, then slap my hand against my leg as my phone buzzes again.

Angoori glances at me, eyes wide and worried. "Are you okay?"

I smile and nod, knowing my face contradicts me. I look up at Etienne, really wanting to know what he's going to do with that stick, and really hoping I can get through the rest of these lessons without constant interruptions.

No such luck.

The buzzing continues as Saulo teaches us capoeira, which is this cool martial arts thing kind of like dance-fighting. It continues as Etienne makes us run the water obstacle course, with stairs made of a giant water wheel, and then paddle through a maze of canals in little wooden canoes. And it continues as Cara has us get out of the canoes to study the wildlife, looking for clues about how the creatures live in and around the water.

No matter how much I try to concentrate, each buzz makes me more nervous and distracted. Finally, I just can't take it anymore. I pull Miriam aside.

"What is it, Coral?" she asks, eyes wide and concerned. "Are the lessons too much?"

"Oh, no. They're awesome." I pull out my phone, which now shows nine new texts. "I haven't been answering them, but I wanted you to know that my Dad has been sending messages all morning."

She sighs. "Jack was always very persistent. What is he saying?"

I scroll through the list but don't open them. "He's mostly asking where I am and why I won't answer. He's threatening to call the police, but he said that earlier too. And oh—" I gulp, not wanting to say it aloud. "He says he's on his way, Miriam. He says he's tracked my phone, and he's assuming I'm with you."

Panicked, I look up at her, but she looks completely calm.

"Now we know," she says. "It will take him some time to get here, so we will finish the training. We may not get another chance during the dry season."

"So, you two know each other?"

"We did, once upon a time."

Obviously, there's a story there, but this doesn't seem like the right time to ask for more. "He's not going to quit," I tell her.

She nods. "And neither will we."

Her eyes flash, which makes me feel stronger, like, whatever happens, we can figure it out. "I guess I should get back to work," I say.

"Most definitely, dear Coral." Her smile shines like a mother's smile, warm and proud.

I watch for a moment, feeling like I could never have enough of a smile like that, and then I put my phone away and hurry back to my friends. It seems like the fight is coming to us, and we need to be ready.

Chapter Twenty

By the next day, everything around me sounds like a ticking clock—the chopping and stirring of our meals, footsteps through the brush, splitting logs for firewood, my beating heart. Miriam told me not to worry about my Dad, and I'm really trying, but my head just won't let go. I know I have big lessons today, though, so I smile and eat my breakfast and join my friends in the classroom.

"Today," Miriam tells us, "we are going to focus our lessons on the individual needs of your communities, since that is where you will each begin your efforts. We will pair up, one guardian to one student, and discuss the needs and obstacles in each place, as well as work with you to understand your individual gifts."

I look at the others, and their excitement lifts my spirits. Once again, I realize, the one with the cushiest life is taking education for granted. Determined not to be that girl, I try to shake off my anxiety and enjoy.

"Hope, you will be with Etienne and explore the soil, as well as to explore planting techniques that make food grow faster; Phonepasit, you will work with Cara and learn about air frequencies and using them to communicate with plants and animals; Angoori will work with Saulo to learn new methods and find increased focus when using fire; and Coral, our water- wielder, will be with me." Miriam scans the group, smiles, then heads over to me. "I hope you are not disappointed that we are a pair," she says.

I sigh. "No, it's good. I feel safe with you."

Her forehead creases. "Do you feel unsafe in other places?"

"I didn't used to," I tell her. "I used to feel like New York City kind of belonged to me, you know? Even though I heard stories, I never really believed there was anything to be afraid of."

"And now you believe otherwise?"

"It just feels like there's so much I don't know. And now my best friend Jasper is in the hospital, and his mom thinks it's because my Dad did something to the water in their neighborhood."

Miriam's eyebrows arch. "Does your father know she believes this?"

I nod. "I told him right before I came here. He said he had nothing to do with it, though, and blamed some environmentalists trying to make him look bad."

She reaches out and grasps my hand. "Being a Pathfinder is not easy, Coral, but you were chosen for a reason. Come, let's sit down." She leads me to a pair of chairs, carved from tree stumps, beneath another huge tree.

I take a seat, suddenly grateful to be in the shade. "Was I chosen because of my mom?" The question feels hot on my tongue, like it will burn whether I ask it or not.

Miriam nods.

"Was she a Pathfinder too?"

"No, she was not. My great-grandmother, Avó was the last Pathfinder, the directions that were given to me by Avó, led me to your mom, Sophia." She smiles. "And we knew, from the time you were very young, that you would be called to the most honorable responsibility."

I open my mouth, suddenly armed with a ton of questions, but she holds up a silencing hand. "I think those stories will have to wait for another day, Coral. There is much I need to teach you before you go home. Conversations about your mother, though I know they feel urgent, can happen in another time and place."

Disappointment floods my body. I've needed answers about my mom for so long. I don't want to wait anymore. "But I've already waited most of my life, Miriam."

Her mouth bends into a sad smile, and she lays her hand over mine. "You won't have to wait much longer, I promise. It's just important for us to prioritize right now."

"Okay," I sigh. "What do I need to learn today?"

"We need to talk about what's going on with the water in New York City. Tell me what you know."

I start with a big shrug. It doesn't feel like I know much of anything. "Well, there's the stuff with Jasper and his mom. And even before he got sick, my Dad didn't want me going to his neighborhood. Honestly, I thought he was being racist or something, but now I think he didn't want me anywhere near his construction site."

Miriam nods. "Is he building elsewhere in the city?"

"I don't know. He never talks about his work anymore. I didn't even know he was doing anything in Jasper's neighborhood until his mom said something."

"Have you noticed any differences in the water generally? Any changes in your apartment, or in public places?"

I stop and think. "Well, the water isn't as clear as it used to be, and we don't drink out of the faucet anymore. My Dad has drinking water delivered. It's also been so hot in the city that it's honestly hard to believe every drop doesn't just evaporate."

She leans forward, her eyes shiny. "See, this is why you were meant to be a Pathfinder. You have an eye for important details."

That makes me smile, though I'm not sure what she means. "Maybe you could tell me what I'm noticing?" I say, hoping that sounds funny instead of dumb.

Miriam chuckles. "Excellent. A good scientist always asks for clarification."

"I am *so* not a scientist," I tell her.

"Not yet." She jumps to her feet and lifts her arms to the skies. "The climate change we discussed earlier is having an effect all over the world, New York City included. It is hotter and raining less and that, combined with bigger and bigger storms, is changing the water cycle as we know it."

I squint up at her. "Changing it how?"

"Come, look." She squats down near the tree and waves me closer. "I want you to take a picture of this standing water." She points to a chain of small pools running between the trees.

After making sure I still have battery—and cringing a little to see it at forty percent—I snap a few pics from different angles. "Okay," I say. "Now what?"

"I want you to come back and compare your photos to the reality throughout the day."

"What am I looking for?"

"I think you'll be surprised at how quickly and drastically the water disappears as the day gets hotter, as well how quickly mosquitoes begin to breed, even in the smallest pools."

148

I nod. "So, the evaporation matters?"

Miriam's eyes get wide. "Oh my, yes. In the old days, they said dilution was the solution to pollution, but it is a bit more complicated today. As you watch the water, think about the impact of evaporation happening, in shorter time frames and greater amounts, all over the world. Every degree matters, and the trend of rising temperatures is undeniable."

A strange heaviness settles over me, and suddenly I understand what people mean when they talk about 'having the weight of the world on your shoulders.' This is serious stuff--stuff most kids don't know to worry about yet.

"Do you know what kind of trees these are?"

I look them up and down, but I have no idea. I do like the way their trunks all intertwine with one another like they know they have to stick together to survive. "If they didn't already have a name, I would call them friendship trees," I tell her with a smile.

Miriam nods. "That fits," she says, "but they do have a name. They are called mangroves and they are natural water filters. They clean the water and make it safe to drink."

"Wow. Nature sure has it all figured out."

She nods, then sighs, long and hard. "If not for human beings, this world would not need saving."

Her sigh makes my heavy heart even heavier. I make a sharp wish that all of this could be different—that my Dad could be the way he used to be, that my mom could still be with us, that the world could be safe and strong. But unlike the wishes I can make with the compass; I don't have the magic to make these happen.

Miriam's hand settles on my shoulder. "Do not lose heart, Coral. The best things take time."

My eyes find hers, and their warmth does make me feel a little better. "You and the Ecomasters are the people my Dad considers his enemies, aren't you? You're the eco-warriors he keeps talking about?" I ask, already way too sure of the answer.

She sighs, long and hard, then nods. "And now that means me too."

She bends down and stares into my face. "Your father is not a bad man, Coral. And I know he loves you very much."

"Could have fooled me," I murmur.

"It hurt him very much when your mother left, and I fear he never recovered."

The questions come back. They twist themselves into a tight ball in my throat. I can't do this without answers, I decide. It's not right for Miriam to expect that. "Why did she do it? Why did she leave us?"

"Come and sit," she says and leads me back to the chairs. When we're seated, she again leans down and looks me in the eye. "Your mother is a very special woman, not a Pathfinder, exactly, but filled with knowing."

"Knowing?"

Miriam nods. "It is an odd combination for a scientist, one who must see to believe, but who also believes intensely in what cannot be seen."

My brain gets a little buzzy. I so want to get what she's saying, but it's not happening. Beneath me, the stump chair feels much too hard, and the air much too warm. "What did she see?" I ask finally.

Sadness washes over her face. "She studied with Avó and the Elders and her heart felt danger on the earth's horizon, Coral, and she knew that your father would ultimately play a role."

"That doesn't make sense. Why go away if there's danger? And why leave me with him? Why not take me with her and let me help?"

"Because you were too young and her work too intense. She knew she needed to leave you for a time. But just for a time."

I shake my head, so wanting to be angry, but then I stop. Whether I like it or not, it makes sense. Being here, on this island, ties it all together.

Miriam places her hands over mine again. "I am sorry I must be the one to tell you this." "It's okay," I tell her. "I get it, even if I hate it." She smiles. "Spoken like a true Pathfinder."

Almost like she planned it, sunshine breaks through the trees all around us. It pierces the ground like shimmering spears, and then seems to pierce me too. It's not just about finding the path, I realize. None of this matters if I don't follow it, if I don't do what I'm meant to do.

I sit up straight, one last question remaining. "Will I get to see my mom soon?"

Miriam's face mirrors the sunshine all around us. "That, my dear, is the good news. The path to healing our world is also the path to your mother."

I exhale hard, almost like I've been holding my breath since my mom left. "Okay, then," I tell her. "I think I'm really ready now."

Chapter Twenty-One

I'm flopping around in my hammock the next morning; something just doesn't feel right. I wonder if I should get up, maybe even find Miriam and the rest of the guardians, but when I glance at my friends, their peaceful faces—and, in Phonepasit's case, light snores—tell me I'm probably worrying about nothing. I pull the pod around me and decide I'll sleep a little longer and then see how things feel.

It seems like my eyes are closed for less than five minutes when a shrill whistle echoes all around us, like a cross between a school fire alarm and a sea of wind chimes. I pull my blanket off my face and sit up. My friends all do the same, and we take turns gaping at each other and staring out into the brush.

"What is happening?" Hope asks, her words hushed but sharp.

Angoori presses her hands to her cheeks. "It doesn't sound good."

Phonepasit just nods, eyes shockingly round.

I want to comfort them, but I can't. I guess my gut was right. And now it's telling me that this probably has something to do with my Dad.

"We must get moving, girls."

I glance up to see Cara hurrying into the hut. "What's going on?" I ask.

"Several of our alarms were tripped. We place them in the forest to alert us if someone, or something, has accessed the portal."

Angoori glances over her shoulder. "What sort of something?" she whispers.

"I'm sure it's a someone," I say, purposely not mentioning my father. I'm not ready to go there yet.

Cara gives me a small nod. "You are probably correct, Coral. We must all take steps to protect the island."

Heart pounding, I jump out of my hammock and put on my shoes. Around me, my friends do the same. "Ready," I say, feeling like this is all my fault. "What do we do?"

"Follow me." Cara dashes out of the hut, and we follow her to the center of camp where Miriam, Etienne, and Saulo gather supplies.

"Good morning, girls," Miriam says. "Today will be much different than the others. It will also be our last day together, I am afraid."

Wow, I think, suddenly a little afraid of my Dad's power. For most kids, a parent showing up would just mean trouble for the kid, kind of like going after a runaway. In my case, though, it's more like he's the problem, one the guardians seem to be worried about in a big way. A wave of guilt washes over me and I shudder, not as thrilled about going home as I should be. I try to shake it off and focus on Miriam's instructions.

153

"To work as quickly as possible, we're going to break into pairs once again," Miriam tells everyone. "We'll each secure a portion of the island and then meet up to say our goodbyes." She stuffs lengths of rope, a knife, and a canteen into her pack and then turns to me. "Ready, Coral?"

I nod, pretty much feeling less ready than I can ever remember, and we head off toward the trees. "Grab that spear," Miriam says to me as we pass the food-prep area, and I gulp as I pick it up. Just what do we have to do? I don't even know if I could swing this thing, and I sure as heck can't use it, or watch anyone use it, against my Dad.

All around me, the forest feels more alive than ever, like the threat woke it up. Instead of just a rush of bird noise, I hear individual calls, an actual conversation. Instead of creatures rustling leaves in the distance, they almost seem to line our path. This makes me smile—I'm part of an army now.

"We need to make sure the traps are camouflaged first, then we'll create some obstacles along the path to camp."

"Traps?" The word makes me a little queasy.

"Oh, nothing overly dangerous. Mostly, we just want to slow down and frustrate anyone who comes near." Miriam glances back at me and smiles. "Usually, people get annoyed and turn back."

My Dad's face fills my mind. He might be a lot of things, but he's never been a quitter. "I'm not sure that'll happen this time."

She slows her pace and matches her steps with mine. "This is not your fault, Coral. Things are happening as they must."

"I'm trying to remember that," I say as we stop in the middle of the path.

"Don't go any farther," Miriam tells me. She bends down and gently touches the earth, pressing like she's testing the weight. "Looks good." She stands and walks into the brush a couple of feet, then waves me forward. "Follow my path exactly," she says.

I move forward, watching only her feet. "What was that?"

"A pitfall trap."

I picture my Dad's angry face as he sits in the bottom of one of those. Not good. "It's not too deep though, right?"

"Only deep enough to make it hard to climb out. Not impossible, of course. Just hard."

I nod and follow her, watching as she shows me how to search for branches of the right length and thickness, how to connect trip wires, and how to make sure the swinging log traps are set and ready. We cover the forest in a semi-circle, and it feels like we set more than two-dozen traps by the time we're done.

"Are all of the others doing this same thing?" I ask.

She nods. "We've divided the area around the island into quadrants, and we each cover one quadrant. That way, intruders have difficulties from every direction."

I take a second to pinch myself, since it suddenly feels like I'm in an Indiana Jones movie or something. If I wasn't so nervous, this would all be crazy cool. "What next?" I ask, a little afraid to know.

Miriam glances at her watch. "Now, we need to meet up with the others."

We're walking back, making sure to avoid all the traps we just created, when a weird rustling sound snakes through the forest, harsh and clunky. Miriam's face tenses, and I realize I'm hearing the sound of boots and machetes.

I study her. "The other guardians?"

She shakes her head and holds a finger to her lips. Then she gestures for me to follow her off the path. We zigzag our way through the trees, away from the sounds. When she spots the rest of the guardians, she nods and points in their direction, then starts walking faster. I hurry to follow, the sound of my pulse in my ears creating a new forest echo.

"Coral!"

I freeze. The voice comes from behind me, and it sounds pretty far away. Miriam stops too and turns to face me. "Don't move," she whispers.

I try to listen, but I can't. I peek over my shoulder and spot my Dad in a small clearing, not even a city block away. Standing with a group of four or five others, he's definitely close enough for me to see the dark line of his frown. "Oh, no," I breathe.

"Stay there," he yells. "I'm coming to get you."

Panic rises like floodwater and, for a second, all I can do is watch him get closer. How did he even know to come here, or to use the water tree? Has he been here before? My heart feels like it's going at hummingbird pace, and I almost can't breathe, but then I remember that it's up to me to do something. I'm a guardian-in-training. It's now my job to protect this place.

I peer across the brush, desperate for an option, then feel Miriam's hand on my shoulder. "We need to go," she hisses.

"Wait," I tell her. "I have an idea."

Stepping forward, but keeping myself hidden behind some bushes, I scan the area. My Dad and his guys are in the middle of the clearing now, but it's the ground beneath them I care about. I reach into my pocket for the compass, and my brain and my palm warm at the same time. This better work, I think, and the compass gets hotter, like it means to reassure me.

"Coral, what are you doing?" Miriam whispers. "We have to get back to the others."

"I can stall them." I hold up my clenched fist and step into a small puddle of water near my foot. "I wish to see quicksand in the clearing," I say, then quiver for a moment, wondering if quicksand is really what I think it is—a hole full of really wet sand. I take a deep breath and hold it, trying to help the wish by picturing what I mean.

At first, it seems like nothing happens. I almost turn and run, but then a frantic yell echoes through the trees. One by one, I see the men fall. Circles take over my Dad's face—two round eyes and a giant yelling mouth—as he stumbles down into the swelling sand under his feet.

For a second, I'm worried, but then I remember I can wish it away in a second. At least I think I can.

When I glance at Miriam, she's grinning. "Very clever, my dear," she says. "Let's hurry to the others. They'll be fine in the sand for at least a few minutes, and then you can wish for some rescue."

I nod, and we take off, the last ones to get back to camp. I'm shocked to see that there's almost nothing left of the vast training camp; it's all been hidden.

"They're close by," I hear her tell the others. "But Coral came up with an ingenious solution. I'm pretty sure they'll be too exhausted to keep searching, but it looks like you all made sure there's nothing to find."

My friends beam, clearly proud of helping, and my heart swells. This is important, and we're making a difference. Not bad for a bunch of kids.

"Time to help your Dad, Coral," Miriam tells me. "They're probably struggling quite a bit by now."

I hurry to pull out the compass, suddenly worried about something bad happening. No matter what, he's still my Dad. After a little searching, I find a water jug and pour some out to make another puddle to stand in. "I wish to flood the quicksand in the clearing," I say, thinking that will dilute the sand and let them swim to shore.

Etienne sets off running. "I will check on them," he calls over his shoulder.

I take a grateful breath. I don't know that I could actually leave without knowing my plan worked.

"Time for goodbyes, girls, remember, learning has only just begun, we'll all be back here very soon" Miriam calls.

"I will miss you, Coral," Angoori says as she wraps me up in her arms.

Hope and Phonepasit sweep in, and soon we're all hugging each other and promising to meet up again soon.

"This has truly changed my life," Phonepasit says.

"I, too, will never be the same." Hope's eyes are damp and shiny.

"You all mean so much to me," I tell them. "Thank you for all you've done. I know it must have seemed insane at first."

We giggle then, because it's so true, then wave the guardians into our group hug.

"They're fine," Etienne calls as he runs back. "Sputtering mad and swimming for dry ground, but they're fine."

"Thank you," I tell him and hurry to give him his hug. "Now I can go."

He nods. "We all need to go. I don't think they're going to head this way, but we don't want to push our luck."

And with that, the wishing begins. One by one, I stand in the puddle and wish my friends home, taking Hope, then returning for Phonepasit, and then for Angoori. I take a deep breath before I wish myself back to New York City, probably because I know that where I'm going isn't anywhere near as magical as where I've been. But then I remember, for the second time that day, that I have a job to do now. I have to protect the world, but I also have to get home, help my city, and save my friend Jasper.

Chapter Twenty-Two

I land right back in my shower, which is still dripping. My new lessons still on my mind, I bristle a little, thinking about how much water that's added up to in the past few days. I guess Henry was a little too confused to worry about making sure the faucet was turned off the right way.

I open the door and step out, whacking my elbow on the glass as I go. "Yowza," I yell, trying to rub the sting away.

A second later, the door flies open. Peeve almost knocks me over, leading with his giant paws and big licking face. "I missed you too, boy," I giggle, so happy my Dad didn't dump him in some doggie daycare while he was gone.

Then my heart flutters a little. If Peeve is here, someone is maybe here with him. Needing to know what I'm up against, I slip out from under his furry body, cross my fingers that things won't go badly, and tiptoe out of my bathroom.

Of course, tiptoeing is not very effective with a huge bear-dog prancing at my side. I try to shush him, but he just keeps wagging his tail and nuzzling me as I try to walk. "Peeve, stop," I say, trying not to sound too harsh.

He barks and wags his whole body at me. I guess I can't blame him. I was gone quite a while.

"Who's there?!" A sharp voice rings out and, as I turn the hallway corner, I crash into something much bigger than Peeve.

"Ummm...sorry," I say. "I didn't know you were still here."

The bodyguard's mouth falls open. He looks so shocked, almost like a cartoon character, and I have to clap my hand over my mouth, so I don't giggle. Poor guy. None of this is his fault.

"How are YOU still here?" He backs up several steps like I might not be real.

"Oh, I haven't been here the whole time," I say. Though it's kind of fun to mess with him, I also realize I need to figure out some kind of story that will make sense.

"But how did you get out of the apartment?"

I fight to keep the grin off my face. "I went out the front door."

He shakes his head, way more times than necessary. "No, I was here. You went into the bathroom, and then you were gone."

"Well, actually, I went into the bathroom to take a shower, but then I got a text about a friend who's in the hospital, and I left in a hurry. I'm sorry I forgot to turn off the water."

The man's mouth falls open, and he stares at me for a long time. "You've been at the hospital for three days?"

"No, but you probably wouldn't believe me if I told you what happened, so let's just be happy I'm back now."

He scowls. "Try me."

I swallow hard, hoping I look honest enough to pull this off. "No, not the whole time. I got lost on the subway on the way back, so I called another friend, who came and found me. By then, my phone was dead, and I didn't have money for the subway, so I had to wait until my friend's mom had a day off and could bring me home."

His eyes narrow into little slits. "Your friend doesn't have a phone?"

I shake my head. "Her family doesn't have a lot of money."

"They don't have a phone in their house?"

Oh, snap. Didn't think about that one. "They haven't been able to pay the bill this month," I say, hoping that will do it.

Henry keeps staring at me, then holds up one palm like we need to stop and start over. "Wait a minute. Your Dad tracked your phone. He said you weren't in the city."

My mouth goes dry. Now what? When in doubt, play dumb, I think. I give him a huge shrug. "I have no idea how those things work. Maybe it doesn't give the right information if the phone is dead."

He looks so confused that it gets hard to keep watching him. I reach down and pet Peeve, needing a distraction. "Thanks for looking after this guy," I say. "I think I'll get him a treat." I lead Peeve to the kitchen, hoping that will be the end of it.

Henry doesn't take the hint. "Have you been in touch with your Dad?"

"Not really." That's totally the truth. And then I fish my phone out of my pocket and hold it up, making sure the case side faces him. "Have to charge this first, remember? Where is he anyway?"

I bite my lip after that one, as pictures of quicksand fill my mind.

"I don't know where exactly, but I know he thought he was going after you."

Peeve gives my leg a head-butt, reminding me that I said the word 'treat,' and I head for the pantry. No need for him to wait any longer. "I'll plug in my phone and text him just as soon as I finish here," I say, trying to sound completely agreeable.

When I look back at him, he's scratching his head and staring at the floor. I know it's not funny, but I still want to chuckle a little. This guy really had no idea what he was in for when he took the job.

"You definitely should," he says. "I'm sure he's very worried."

"I'll take care of it, I promise," I tell him. "I sure don't want him to worry."

The man nods though not like he means it and walks out of the kitchen. "That was a close one, boy," I whisper to Peeve. "I think I better do as much as I can before Dad gets back. Seems like things are going to be pretty complicated from now on."

Chapter Twenty-Three

The best thing about my situation at home is that Henry is now officially scared of me. He looks at me like I'm some kind of teenage witch—which, as the owner of a magical compass, I guess I might be—and, though he checks on me now and then, he pretty much lets me do my own thing. That's really saying a lot, because

I know he must be getting the same cranky texts I've been getting from my Dad.

I'm pretty sure my Dad doesn't buy my story about being in the city the whole time, lost and without a phone, but I'm also pretty sure he didn't get a good enough look at me or Miriam to trust what he saw. His texts since then don't mention the Amazon or the island at all, and that tells me he's just not sure. It also makes me really glad I didn't respond to any of them, and SUPER-DUPER glad I got annoyed with Jasper a few months ago and turned off the little setting that shows people when their texts have been read. That was the luckiest thing of all.

Well, maybe the second luckiest, since I texted Jasper's sister this morning and found out he's out of the hospital. Reading that made me smile and get teary at the same time. It also told me what I'm going to do with this day of freedom, since I know my Dad will be traveling until after I'm in bed tonight.

"I'll be back in a while," I tell Henry. Peeve follows me as I walk, clearly bummed that he doesn't get to come with me, but I've already given him extra treats and explained that we need to let Jasper get all the way better before the dog visits begin.

Henry frowns. "Where are you going?"

I smile. It feels great to be able to tell the truth, even if it's only for a day. "My friend is out of the hospital and I'm going to see him."

"Where does he live?"

"East Harlem." I head to the kitchen for a bottle of water. As I walk, I check my pocket for the compass. I've gotten a little obsessive about never letting it out of my sight—or touch— but who can blame me? Plus, I have a little experiment in mind for today.

"You're not supposed to go out alone," Henry calls.

Peeve barks in response. He does NOT like anyone raising his voice at me. I smile and bend down to reward him with an ear scratch. I don't think there's ever been a better best dog friend.

Henry appears in the doorway. "Umm..." He eyes Peeve, then looks at me. "I'm going with you."

I shrug and then smile, hoping I don't look as nervous as I feel. "If you want to sit and listen to middle schoolers talk for hours, I guess that's up to you."

"We can't be gone for hours. Your father will worry."

"But I haven't seen Jasper in forever. We have a ton to talk about."

Henry frowns and cocks his head. "I'll give you an hour. That should be plenty."

My turn to frown. This is not going well. "What about Peeve? I'm not sure if Jasper's mom will let him in the house. Germs, you know."

"Which is why we leave him at home."

I make a big deal out of sighing. "He doesn't like to be left alone. If he chews up the furniture, we're both in trouble."

Expression skeptical, Henry looks back and forth between Peeve and me. "You never leave him alone?"

"I try not to, and I definitely don't give him the run of the house."

"Put him in your room then." Henry walks back into the living room, eyes searching. "Just let me grab my coat while you do that."

My grin stretches wide. That's the moment I've been waiting for. Pretending to toss a ball Peeve's way, I send him running out of the kitchen and down the hall. "Hey, can you grab him and put him in, Henry? You're closer."

He grunts, but I hear Peeve's collar jingle as he grabs him. Feeling triumphant but guilty, I tuck my keys in my pocket and give a wave no one can see. "Bye, Peeve," I whisper and hurry out the door.

In the elevator, I have a wobbly moment when I think about strolling right past Mr. Dobbins, but I decide to just keep the bravery rolling. If I slipped one guard, I can slip another. By the time the doors open, I stroll out like I'm the one paying the bills.

"Miss Marchant," he says with a nod when he sees me.

"Hi, Mr. Dobbins." I swallow hard, pushing down all the explanations I would usually give him. Just walk, I tell myself, and I do, ignoring the weight of his eyes on my back.

When I get down the block, I turn left and head toward another apartment building a little way down. This one has a fountain in a small side court just off the sidewalk. I walk over to it and sit down on its edge like I need a rest. Then, when I don't see anyone nearby, I slip my flip-flopped feet over the side and put them in the water.

My temples flutter as I sit there, compass in hand, and I'm not sure why I'm so nervous. If my experiment doesn't work, it doesn't work, I tell myself. Miriam never said the compass was only for Pathfinder business, and maybe this *is* Pathfinder business. I mean, I want to check on my friend, but I also want to find out what I can about my Dad and whatever he's done in East Harlem. That might count.

"I wish to see Jasper," I say finally.

Around my feet, the water churns like the fountain doubles as a whirlpool tub. I close my eyes, even though I want to watch, and try to make myself calm down. It's not like I'm doing anything wrong. Am I?

The answer comes when I land, ankles-deep, in a kiddie pool. I look down at the pale blue plastic, covered with happy orange, yellow, and purple fish, and grin. It's almost like the water has a sense of humor.

"Where am I?" I mutter, then glance around me for clues. It's a small backyard, fenced on all sides, with a wooden gate to the alley in back. It can't be Jasper's yard, I think, since no one in his family is small enough for a pool like this. My heart pounds, and it hits me that I could get in big trouble if someone sees me out here.

I jump out of the pool and run out into the alley, trying to figure out if anything looks familiar. As I close the gate, I glance up at the second floor of the building next door and spot a clue. Through one of the windows, I see a LeBron James poster on the wall next to one of Harry Potter, and my whole body relaxes. That's Jasper, all right.

166

Feet squishing in my shoes, I run down the alley and go around the block. Within minutes, I'm standing at his front door. I knock and wait, then knock again. The door finally opens, and Jasper's sister peeks out at me.

"Hey there," she says. "He's upstairs. I didn't tell him you texted, so this will be a good surprise."

"Awesome." I step inside and take off my drippy flip-flops.

Sonya looks down at my bare feet and tilts her head.

"I wasn't paying attention and walked through a big puddle," I tell her. "That's weird. I haven't seen standing water around here in ages."

I bite my lip, hoping it won't be a big deal. "Can I go up?"

She smiles and nods, and I'm on my way. I take the steps a couple at a time, happier and happier as I go. When I get to Jasper's doorway, it hits me how much I've missed him. And how lucky we all are that he's okay.

"Look at you," I say, "lounging around like nothing ever happened."

He glances up from his phone, eyes a little glazed from what I assume are nonstop rounds of that Minecraft game he's addicted to, and flashes a huge grin. "It's about time you came to see me," he says. His voice is almost all squeak this time, but I make myself keep a straight face.

"Dude. I came to see you. They wouldn't let me in."

"I know. My mom told me. I was actually really impressed you made it all the way there on the subway."

"Hey, what are friends for?" I push his legs over and sit down on the end of his bed. "So, you're feeling good?"

Jasper nods, then shrugs. "A lot better, yeah. Still a little weak, and I don't feel much like eating, but it's nothing like it was."

"Were you scared?"

He blinks a few times, then nods again. "Yeah. Definitely."

His face gets a little sad, and I feel bad for asking the question. "Well, that doesn't matter now," I tell him. Now that I've seen him, the things I need to ask him start pressing on me from the inside. "So... what did they tell you happened?"

All the lines in his face bend down toward his chin, eyes and mouth frowning together. "It was something in the water. Something that shouldn't have been there."

"The doctor said that?"

He nods. "They did tests."

I suck in a deep breath. There it is. The thing I haven't really been wanting to hear. "Did your mom talk to you about my Dad?"

He nods again, and it seems hard for him to look at me.

"It's okay," I tell him. "I've learned a lot in the past few days, and a lot of it doesn't make my Dad look so good."

Jasper sighs. "Sorry. That must stink."

"Sure does." I lean forward, really wanting to tell him about everything—the compass, what the water does, the countries I've seen and the friends I've made, being a Pathfinder—but something makes my lips stay pursed. What if it's too much for him? And what if he doesn't believe me? I can't risk it.

"Can I ask you about the water? Did you notice anything different about it right before you got sick?"

Jasper throws off the covers and sits up, making a pretzel out of his legs. His red and gold Harry Potter pajamas make me smile. He's definitely a Gryffindor.

"It did taste a little funny. Not bad, just different. And I remember noticing a smell, but it never occurred to me that it came from the water."

"And that was just on the day you got sick?"

He shakes his head. "No, I think I noticed it for a few days. It seems like it started happening when the water pressure changed. Not much would come out, even with the faucet turned all the way."

I listen and, as he talks, I think about what I learned in Ecomasters training. I think about where New York City's water comes from and how it gets to our houses, and I think about how the water is impacted by whatever happens around it. The back of my neck starts to tingle.

168

What in the world is my Dad doing? Is he taking the water away from the city? Is he adding something to it? Is the heatwave making it worse?

"Is the water still like that?" I ask.

Jasper scowls. "Yep. I was hoping it would be better when I got home, but it's the same. We're all afraid to drink it, and my mom makes me use my mouth guard from soccer when I take a shower, so I don't get anything in my mouth."

My shoulders sag. Man, this is bad. I need to do something.

I look my friend in the eye. "I'm really glad you're okay, and I'm really sorry that my Dad has anything to do with this."

He reaches over and puts his hand on my arm. "You can't help what your Dad does, Coral. I know you would never hurt anyone."

The clouds over my heart lift a little. It's funny how you can know you didn't do anything wrong and still feel responsible. And maybe that's how I need to feel so I'll be brave enough for what comes next.

"Thanks, Jasper," I say. "It's really good to see that you're okay."

He smiles and nods, then takes his hand back before it gets weird, thank goodness. "Can you hang out for a while?" he asks.

I sigh. Man, do I wish I could say yes. "I can't today. I have something really important to take care of. But maybe I can come back another day this week?"

"That would be great. We could even go to the garden if you want."

"Sign me up," I tell him and get to my feet. I take one more look around me—the little pieces of personality on my best friend's bedroom walls—and grin back at LeBron and Harry, then study the NASA poster and the framed pictures he took with his International Space Station app. He's a cool kid, and I almost lost him. Nothing like that can happen. I just won't let it.

"See you soon, Jasper." I wave and walk out the door, ready to do whatever it takes.

Chapter Twenty-Four

It's really quiet when I get back to the apartment, which is weird. Throat dry and stomach fluttery, I press the front door closed, slip off my shoes, and tiptoe across the foyer floor. My biggest worry is that my Dad found some supersonic jet to fly him home from the Amazon in record time. I'm also a little concerned about Peeve, because he NEVER misses a chance to greet me when I come home.

When I turn the corner between the kitchen and the living room, the sight makes me put on the brakes. Henry is there, shoes off and suitcoat tossed over a chair, sound asleep on the couch. Wow, I think. Must be nice to have his job. Then I realize that he probably didn't sleep much after it seemed like I disappeared into thin air. He probably got majorly chewed out by my Dad too. I guess his job might not be so great after all.

But now I don't know what to do. Should I wake him up and let him know I'm back? It seems like the right thing, but the idea of him breathing down my neck as I do what I have to do already annoys me. I decide to write him a note—back in the apartment, didn't want to wake you, blah, blah—and leave it on the coffee table in front of him.

Next, I go look for Peeve. He's been quiet for much too long. When I see my closed bedroom door, though, it all makes sense. Henry didn't want to worry about him while he took his nap.

Breathing a sigh of relief, I open the door to find my buddy, also napping, a big black ball in the middle of my hot pink bed. He sits up and shakes his head a few times, then bounds to the floor and jogs over to me.

"Hey, boy. How's it going? Have a nice nap?"

He chuffs and nuzzles my leg, then sits in front of me like he's waiting for instructions.

"I have things to do," I tell him, "but you can come and sit by me." I flop down at my desk and start up my computer, needing information fast. Who knows how long Henry will sleep? And maybe I don't have the whole day to work with before my Dad gets home.

Within a few minutes, I've printed a list of phone numbers, every single organization I can think of that might care about water in New York City. I mean, it's a big place, so this has to be a big deal, right?

After a deep, deep breath, I call the first number.

"Water Department," a woman says.

"Um...yeah...hello. I would like to report a problem with the water."

"What sort of problem?"

"Well, it tastes a little funny, and maybe smells bad too."

"It *maybe* smells bad?"

I sit up a little straighter. This might be harder than I thought. "I mean, it's not horrible, but sometimes I get a little whiff of a bad smell."

"What's your name? And how old are you?"

Oh, crumbs. I guess I forgot I sound like a thirteen-year-old. "I don't want to make a report or anything," I tell her. "I just thought you should know something's not right with the water in East Harlem."

The woman sighs. "What's the address?"

A deep thumping starts in my chest. I should have known they'd want details. "Just check it out." I say. "East Harlem. Pleasant Avenue." I feel a little weird about naming Jasper's street, but I want them to look in the right place.

"And what—"

I end the call. That's enough info for now.

Next to me, Peeve whines a little. I reach down and scratch his ears. "I'll take you out soon, buddy, I promise. Just let me finish this."

Next, I try City Hall. They should care, right? I keep repeating that to myself as I dial. "City Hall, how may I direct your call?"

Gulp. How should I know? "Umm...I'm not sure."

"Which department do you need?"

"Ahh...water, I guess?"

"I would suggest calling the water department directly."

"What about construction? Is that a department?"

"Like the housing authority?"

Whoa. This is complicated. I take a deep breath and try to sound older. "Yes, that sounds right. Thank you."

There's no response, just more ringing. As I wait, I decide I need to make this simple. "New York Housing Authority." "Yes, hello. I just want to report a problem with the construction in East Harlem." "What's the problem?"

"Something's wrong with the water. Pleasant Avenue. Marchant Construction. Check it out."

I hang up, heart pounding, and flop back in my chair. Who knew phone calls could be so terrifying? Just as I start to breathe a little easier, my phone rings. I look down at the number, and it's the one I just called. My heart straight-up stops this time.

"Crap, Peeve. What do I do?"

He just stares up at me, eyes full of 'don't ask me, I'm just a dog' energy.

Hand shaking, I push the 'decline' button. I almost block the number, so they can't call me again, but then I decide I might need it again later if this plan doesn't go my way. *Gotta be brave if you're gonna save the world, kid.*

"Yikes," I mumble, and then think maybe two calls will be enough.

At that, my head explodes with pictures—Jasper in his pajamas, Miriam scommunicating with pink dolphins and turtles in the rainforest, my new friends. The last one, my mom, seals the deal. I can't stop. This is too important, and it's what I'm meant to do.

After that, the calls get easier. I make three more, to the city's environmental protection agency, to the sanitation department, and the city's construction council. I talk as fast as I can each time, and I put a piece of paper in front of my mouth to disguise my voice a little bit. I don't know if any of it works but, by the time I hang up for the last time, at least I feel like I made a good start. Remembering my lesson about mangrove trees cleaning the water, I begin to wonder if there are trees which might be able to help to cool the city and found a really exciting campaign called Million Trees NYC, so I made one last call to learn more about how kids like me can help with planting and care for local trees. That's it! I don't know if any of it works but, by the time I hang up for the last time, at least I feel like I made a good start.

I sigh, and plop down on my bed. I reach my hands downward, and into my pocket. A good start. But telephones aren't the only way to communicate, as I recently discovered...

What if I could communicate directly with the water? If the water is tapping into and connecting the consciousness of humans, can I tap into the consciousness of water and speak to it directly?

I turn the thought over in my mind, "Water is what unites us – and water is how we will communicate." I shrug to myself, thinking, well, what have I got to lose?

Out loud, both hands on my compass I say, "Water is what unites us – and water is how we will communicate." In my mind's eye, I hold my intention to connect with water as strong and steady as I can, staying in a space of gratitude.

I wait, feeling awkward, but stay with it.

I 'hear' a soft murmur, and what comes isn't in words, but in visions. My mouth must be wide open, because I don't know what I expected, but this is beyond.

I "see" the underground water system of the city, and I see in flashing imagery where it is "sick", and where it is flowing healthy. There's a pulsing, muddy energy near where Jasper and his mom live. I receive communication in a felt-sense way, like a big hug – a feeling, unmistakable. Ancient, powerful, a field that totally envelops me. It seems to say, gentle yet firm: "you're doing the work above the ground; I'll handle the work below the ground."

Teamwork. I smile to myself, amazed.

Shaking my head, I take a deep breath. And feel a renewed sense of mission and purpose. This may be hard – and it's all been wild – and challenging at times, but man, is it worth it.

"Now we wait," I say to Peeve, who somehow looks relieved. "I promised you a walk, didn't I, boy?"

His tail wags like it means to come right off.

"Okay, then," I say. "Let's go."

I walk him out toward the door, past a still-sleeping Henry. The dude is not the best bodyguard I've ever seen, but I'm not complaining. I take a second to jot a little P.S. on his note, and then Peeve and I head out. Might as well enjoy my last little bits of freedom. Who knows what might happen tomorrow?!

Chapter Twenty-Five

My alarm goes off at seven the next morning, a little earlier than I usually like, but I hate the idea of my Dad storming in and waking me up. I mean, maybe he'll be chill, but after flying around the world for nothing, I kind of doubt it.

Peeve grunts like I've personally offended him when I move and, clearly not cool with the early-rising plan, he dives deeper under the covers and starts snoring all over again. "That's okay, boy," I tell him. "I'll take one for the team this time."

I slide out of bed, prepared to do a little spying around the apartment. If Henry is gone, that'll be a big clue, though I also know my Dad might keep him here while he sleeps. I decide to check the couch first, then look on the foyer table for keys before I check my Dad's bedroom.

As soon as I open my bedroom door, though, I get my answer. It sounds like he's standing in the hallway yelling, but when I step out, I see that he's just screaming that loud from his office. Taking like six deep breaths, I move around the corner and into the living room. The couch is empty but, as angry as my Dad sounds, I can't decide if that's a relief or not.

"What do you mean, *under investigation*?" he bellows. I freeze. Oh, man. Oh, holy, moly man! I think my phone calls did something. "Well, what did they say?"

I wait, wanting to know too.

"They've halted ALL the work?"

A gasp bubbles up, but I don't let it pass. It's hard to believe I did this. Did I do this? "For how long?"

His tone drops a little, so I inch closer.

"That's just unacceptable. You tell them to stay there. I'm on my way."

Something slams against his desk, and I don't want to know what it is. Still holding my breath, I stop, turn, and run back to my bedroom. I close my door carefully, then leap back into my bed. Peeve gives a little half-bark but then snuggles up to me like I never left.

"Thanks, buddy," I whisper. "I think I'm going to need those cuddles."

The words have barely left my lips when my door flies open. I sit up, trying to look sleepy.

"I have to leave, Coral," my Dad barks, not quite yelling anymore, but still pretty loud.

"Um...okay. Is something wrong?"

He shakes his head, over and over like he can't stop. "I have to go to the jobsite. There's a problem."

"What kind of problem?"

A frown takes over his whole face. "Honestly, I have no idea. Some bureaucratic BS." He stops and looks at me, almost like he's seeing me for the first time. "You and I have a lot to talk about."

I just blink at him. It doesn't feel safe to say anything.

"I expect you to be here when I get back."

That doesn't sound good. I slip a little farther under my comforter, as if the butterflies could protect me. "When will that be?"

"I have no idea. Your best bet is not to leave."

"What if Peeve needs to go out?"

"Then you follow the twenty-minute rule, just like before."

I sigh, then press my comforter to my mouth, hoping he didn't hear. I sure don't need to make this worse. "Okay," I say quietly.

"Henry will be here in about an hour." He walks toward the door.

"Why do I need Henry if you're back?"

My Dad stops like he smacked into a wall, then turns to look at me. "Things are not getting better, Coral. In fact, with what's going on today, I'm worried that they're about to get much, much worse. You and I have a lot to figure out and, even though Henry has a lot to learn about dealing with kids, I feel confident you'll both do better from now on."

I watch him as he talks, at least twelve different feelings pushing and shoving inside me. He really does look worried, but I don't know if that's because of me or his business. For a second, I want to be little again, to go back to the time when I didn't know bad things could happen or the earth was in danger. But then I realize that this day would still have to come, and it wouldn't be any easier the second time around.

"So, we understand each other?" he asks.

I nod, but it feels like the biggest lie I've ever told, which, considering the past week or so, is saying a lot.

"I'll see you later." He hurries out the door, smacking the frame twice as he passes by.

"Can't wait," I whisper, suddenly hoping that whatever he has to do on the construction site takes a lot longer than expected.

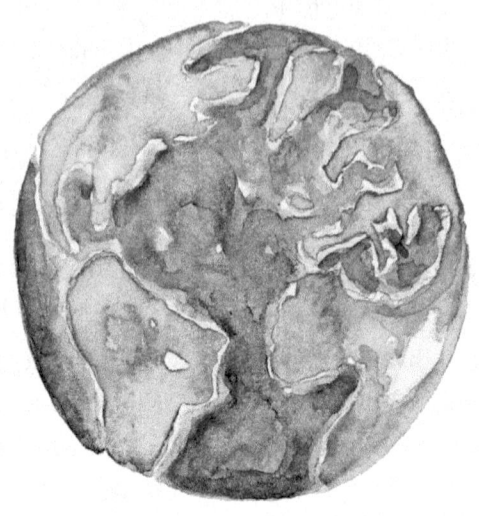

Chapter Twenty-Six

As soon as I hear the door slam, I push Peeve out of bed and take him outside. I do everything just as I'm supposed to, saying hello to Mr. Dobbins and telling him I'll be quick and then only staying out as long as it takes for Peeve to do his thing. When I get back to the apartment, though, it's time for the real plan.

I'm not going to waste time walking through the city when I can get there faster, I decide, and right now, the where I need most is Miriam's house. There's so much I need to tell her. And so much I need her to tell me.

I wolf down a cranberry muffin and some juice while Peeve finishes his breakfast, and then I stow him in my room. When Henry gets here, if I'm

178

not already back, I want it to look like I'm in the shower. To really sell it, I set up my tablet to play music, so it sounds like I'm really enjoying the water. As long as I'm gone no longer than an hour, I should be able to pull it off.

After locking the bathroom door and hanging my bathrobe on its hook—definitely don't want to walk out in sopping wet clothes—I turn the shower on, but not at full blast. No reason to waste any more water than necessary. Then I step inside, close my eyes, and make my wish.

Just like always, the stretching feeling comes, but by the time I land, I feel more like a medicine ball dropped from a balcony. Water splashes up and over my head, and I spit and gurgle as I open my eyes. What the heck?

I'm standing in a rain barrel on a small patio. Judging by the number of plants surrounding me, I'm pretty sure that patio belongs to Miriam, thank goodness. I climb out of the barrel, which, as a short person, isn't easy, and I end up making a tiny tidal wave all over Miriam's pavers.

When I pound on her door, there's no answer. I start to worry, since I don't have much time, and I don't know how I'll get through the conversation with my Dad unless I get to talk to Miriam first. I pound a few more times, then look around me. Though there's no easy path out of her backyard and to her front door, and it looks like escaping means I'll have to climb a fence, I decide that's what has to happen.

I walk over, see that the wall is even taller than I thought, and look around for something to stand on. A big plastic bucket stands near the plants, and I grab that and flip it over near the fence. I perch on it, with no idea what to do next. It honestly feels like the wall is growing as I stand there. There's no other way to get of the yard and around the house, though, so I have to figure this out.

"Coral?"

The voice startles me, and I lose my balance and tumble onto the grass.

Miriam grins at me from the doorway. "Why on earth are you standing on a bucket in my yard, dear?"

I smile back, so happy to see her. "It doesn't matter," I say, jumping to my feet. "You're here, and now I don't have to."

"Fair enough. Won't you come in?" She swings the door wide.

"Thanks." I hurry inside, then follow her into her office. "You won't believe what's happened," I tell her, before I even sit down.

"I'm sure I will believe you but do tell."

I look around me as I take a seat. I wouldn't have thought she could squeeze even one more plant into this room, but I'm pretty sure she has. The air reminds me of the Amazon, though, and it instantly makes me feel calm and focused.

"So, Jasper is better and home from the hospital."

"That's wonderful."

"And the tests show the water made him sick."

Miriam goes a little pale. "That's horrible. We must do something." It literally feels like my smile will break my face. "I already did." She raises an eyebrow and waits.

"I knew I couldn't just wait and see. Other kids and old people are getting sick and some may not be as lucky as Jasper. So, I called all around the city and made complaints about the water and the construction my Dad is doing, and I even found a campaign for planting trees in the city, which hopefully can help. And…I…spoke with the water"

My grin only gets bigger when her mouth drops open. "Did you now?" she says.

"Yep. And it worked."

"I saw the city, and where the water was 'sick'…and the water spoke in feelings and visions, not in words. I received a message: that our work above the ground in rectifying our communities was the 'teamwork' that we need now more than ever on this planet. It's how we can help our planet, and each other."

She leans forward, eyes wide.

"I woke up to my Dad yelling on the phone about an investigation and being shut down until further notice. He's there now, trying to sort it all out."

"Well, let's hope he's not able to do that." She reaches out and squeezes my hand. "Well done, dear Coral. Very well done. I'm extremely proud of you."

My heart lifts like a helium balloon. Those are exactly the words I need to hear. "I honestly can't believe it made a difference. I just knew I had to try something."

"You have the instincts of a Pathfinder, that is for certain."

"Today, I feel like one," I tell her.

A shadow passes over her face, and I feel some of my worry come back. "This is a success, to be sure, but it is likely only temporary," she says. "Our world is large and troubled, and many battles lay ahead."

I nod, not sure what to say.

She squeezes my hand again. "I do feel much better about our chances with you and your friends on our team."

That pushes my spirits back up. "I do too, Miriam. And I feel really honored. I know we can do this."

"Indeed, we can, my dear."

I jump up and hug her, feeling as close to having a mom back as I have in lots of years. "Thanks, Miriam. That means everything."

She pushes me back, just a bit, grasps my arms, and looks me in the eye. "I will always be here for you, Coral. And someday, your mother will join us."

The throbbing ache, the one that never stops and never goes away, intensifies, reminding me of what I need from her. "When is someday, Miriam?"

Her expression crumbles a little, and I can tell I'm not going to like what she's about to say. "I don't have an answer for you, dear one."

"But I've figured things out and traveled all over the world and mostly kept my Dad off our trail. Isn't that enough to at least see her for a few minutes?" I reach into my pocket and pull out the compass. "If I wish for her, right now, will this thing take me to her?"

Miriam shakes her head, and every back and forth pinches my heart. "I'm sorry, child. It doesn't work that way. We use the compass to serve the planet's purpose, not our own."

I nod. My brain feels like it already knew that answer. "But I'm closer to seeing her?" I manage, needing to walk away with something, however small.

"Oh, *yes*," she says, eyes shining. "Sophia waits for you, Coral. The right time will come."

My eyes fill up so that I almost can't see her, and I hug her again to hide the tears. "I can't wait for that day. I really can't."

She sighs. "I know your mother is counting the minutes as well." She wraps me up in another hug and I close my eyes and lean into it, almost feeling better.

When I open my eyes, the clock glares at me over her shoulder, and I give a little gasp. "Oh, no! Can I use your shower, Miriam? I have to get home!"

We both burst into giggles. What a funny life this has become.

"Follow me," she says, and I do.

I have no idea what I'm going back to, but I feel a whole lot readier to keep fighting than I did before.

Chapter Twenty-Seven

Forty-seven minutes. That's how long I'm gone, according to the clock in my bathroom. I turn off the water and, as weird and backward as it seems, get undressed before I step out of the shower. I make a mental note to come back and collect my wet clothes later, then pull the shower curtain closed on the whole mess and slip into my bathrobe.

The warm fuzziness calms me a little, and I stand in front of the mirror, combing my hair and taking lots of deep breaths. After a few minutes, I turn off my music and press my ear to the door. All quiet. Wouldn't it be something if I even beat Henry back to the apartment?

Not ready to believe I'm home free, I tiptoe out into the hallway and listen again. Nothing. I move closer to the living room, take a deep breath, then peek around the corner. Oh my gosh. Nothing.

All the air rushes out of me in one big wave of relief. I've been having a lot of fun the last several days, but almost nothing has happened the way I expected. Don't get me wrong, I like surprises, but this feels pretty good too. To celebrate, I decide to treat myself to a cup of cocoa.

When I step into the kitchen, my heart stops along with my feet. My Dad stands at the island, his back to me, and it looks like he's just staring down at the speckled granite. I don't know what to do. My first instinct is to back up and head for my bedroom, but as I lift my foot, his head moves, just a little.

"How was your shower?" he says.

I chew my cheek, not sure how to answer. He never asks me that. Is he saying he knows I wasn't really showering? Or does that mean he buys it?

"Umm...good. Thanks." I swallow hard and step closer to the island. "How are things at the jobsite?"

"Not so good." He wraps his hand around the coffee mug in front of him. I'm not sure why it makes me feel better to know that he was looking at something besides the kitchen counter, but it does.

"Can I help?" I bite my lip and wish that one back as soon as I say it. That's a dumb offer from the person who caused the problem.

My Dad looks up at me, eyes tired, then looks down again. "I don't think so." "I thought you'd be gone longer," I say.

"I have to go back."

"Oh."

His eyes find me again. "I'm going to have to be gone a lot in days to come. We have problems I'm not sure how to solve."

"Sorry, Dad," I tell him, and it hits me that I really am. I don't really know what he's up to, and I at least want to believe he thinks he's doing the right thing. I just happen to know he's hurting people, and the earth, and I can't let that happen.

"Thanks." He takes a big drink from his cup, then spends a lot of time trying to set it back on the counter in exactly the same place. When the handle is exactly parallel to the edge of the counter, he looks up at me again. "I came home so we could talk."

"Oh. Sure," I say, trying to sound casual. "Do you care if I make some cocoa while we do that?"

"Go ahead."

I grab what I need, so happy to have something else to concentrate on. For a second, I think about warming the milk on the stove instead of the microwave, since it will take longer, but then it seems like a bad idea.

"So, where were you?" he asks quietly.

The hand pouring the milk freezes. "I was in the shower," I say carefully. He sighs. "Not today. When you were gone."

I give my own version of a sigh. "Oh, that! It was just like I told you in my texts. I got lost on the subway, and then my phone died, but I found my way to a friend's house, and then I—"

"I saw you, Coral."

All the blood in my body rushes to my feet, and I put the milk and my mug on the counter, so I don't drop them. "In the subway?" I manage.

His face suddenly looks like a mask. "In the Amazon."

Okay, here it is. THE moment. If I can't get him to believe me, my days as a Pathfinder might be over. Luckily, I think my face already looks super confused, so I have that going for me.

"Is that where you were? The Amazon?" I ask.

"You know that's where I was."

I can't move. It takes every bit of my energy to keep my expression from changing. "Because you just told me."

He exhales hard, then bends down and presses his face into his hands. When he looks up at me again, I finally feel like my Dad is home. "You really don't know what I'm talking about?"

Oh boy. THE moment just got bigger. Tears rush to my eyes, because this suddenly feels like too much, like no fun. I don't want to lie to my Dad. But I don't want my Dad to do bad things.

A soft puff of air moves over me, like the wind shifting before a storm moves in, but lighter, hopeful instead of threatening. *Trust that everything can be fixed, Coral. Listen to your heart and follow your path.* The words ride on this breeze like faraway music and, deep within, I hear my mother's voice.

I blink until I can see him clearly, then try to find my own voice. "I'm sorry this is happening, Dad. And I'm sorry I worried you and made you upset."

There. That's all true. Now maybe we can get to the fixing.

He stares at me for a really long time. I want to look away so bad, but it almost feels like he needs me to stay with him, like he's remembering something he used to know. Or maybe that's just what I want him to be doing.

"Come here," he says finally and holds out his arms.

I walk around the island and hug him. It feels nice, like now I'm the one remembering something I used to know, but maybe also like I'm saying goodbye to something I wish I didn't have to lose.

He pats my back and steps away. "I have to go back to work."

"Okay. Will Henry be here soon?"

"No. I need him at the office."

That makes me look harder at him, and a little shiver runs through me. Is this a trick?

My Dad puts his mug in the sink and then steps in front of me once again. "I wasn't kidding about the danger out there, Coral, "he says. "But my way of protecting you doesn't seem to be working."

"I'll be careful," I tell him, trying not to look stunned.

"This is not me giving you permission to run the city. Are we clear?"

I nod, wondering what he might think about a quick trip around the world.

"And I expect you to keep in touch."

"Got it." I give him a thumbs-up.

He kisses the top of my head, grabs his keys off the foyer table, and disappears out the door. I stand there, more surprised than I've been in a long time. I'm not sure how I feel about it all yet, but I think maybe some time in the park with good friends might get me back on track.

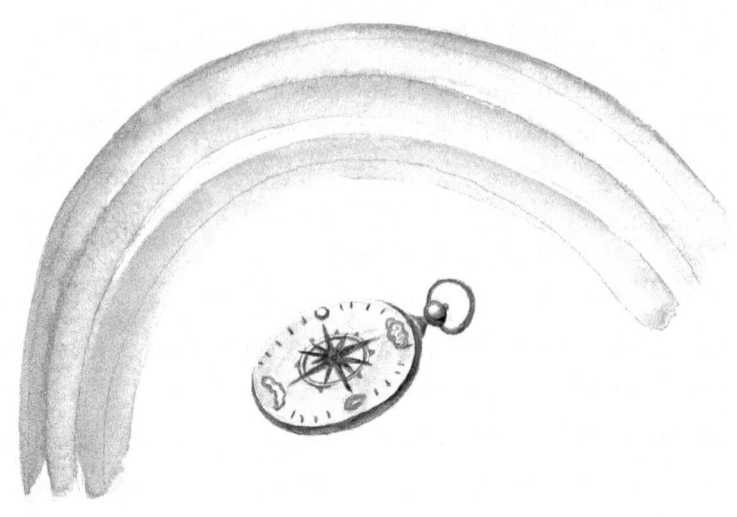

Chapter Twenty-Eight

After quick calls to Hope, Phonepasit, and Angoori, Peeve and I leave for Central Park. We agreed they'd make their wishes in an hour, which gives us time for a good long walk and a nice game of fetch. Mr. Dobbins looks a little cranky as we pass by, but I decide that's not my problem and keep walking. Man, it feels good not to have to check in with him.

Peeve feels pretty good too, I can tell. I have to keep slowing him down as we walk. He's not the one with a giant weight on his back—a pack full of picnic snacks and drinks for my friends—and he clearly doesn't understand why we don't just sprint to the park.

"Easy, boy," I tell him when the crowds get a little bigger. We don't need to make anyone else angry on our way to have fun.

He sees the park entrance, though, so it's like he doesn't hear me at all. In seconds, I'm racing down the sidewalk, completely at the mercy of my giant bear-dog. People grumble as we rush past, and I try to smile and apologize to them all. And then one erases my smile.

"You need to be careful," a scowling blonde woman in a royal blue windbreaker hisses as she nears me.

"I'm so sorry. He's just excited."

She shakes her head and pushes past. "I'm not talking about the dog," she says.

"What?" I pull Peeve to a stop and turn to look at her, expecting her to have more to say. But she's gone. Like really gone. Not a hint of blonde hair or blue nylon anywhere around.

Peeve barks, clearly not enjoying the delay, and then takes off again. Arms flailing, I follow him and try to put the woman out of my mind.

When we get to the lake, a whole buffet of sticks waits in the hay-like grass for Peeve, and we run around chasing them and each other like it's the first day of Spring. It's not, though, and when I'm about as hot and sweaty as I can handle, I flop down into the grass. Peeve joins me, and I make a new game out of squirting water into his mouth from my water bottle.

Finally, the roaring sound I've grown to love fills my ears. I look out at the lake, just in time to see the beginnings of a graceful waterspout. It twirls and dances and, one by one, my friends tumble out of the water and onto the shore. Angoori's expression is the best of the three, looking terrified AND thrilled as she rides the magical wave.

I peek over my shoulder, suddenly worried that we might have attracted a crowd, but there's just one confused-looking guy, maybe high school age, shaking his head like he might be going crazy and urging his dog to stop sniffing and walk. I chuckle, relieved, then give each of my friends one of the hand towels I packed—at least their faces can be dry, even if their clothes have to be wet. Then we sit down to our picnic of pretzels, cheese, and chocolate-covered raisins.

"You are like a fairy godmother, Coral," Hope says as she nibbles. "First you teach us to wish, then you spoil us with treats."

Angoori giggles. "I have never been to a birthday party, but this is how I imagine it would be."

My mouth falls open a little, but then I remember how different our lives are. "I will make sure you have a proper American birthday party someday, Angoori. This is just a little hint of what's to come."

Her eyes get big and she grins. "I look forward to that day."

"It is good to see you all again." Phonepasit crosses her legs and leans forward. "I was worried, when we said goodbye at the EcoMasters camp, that it might be a long time before we were together again, if ever."

The others nod, and I decide it's time to tell them what's been happening here, and what a difference we've made in my city. I try not to paint my Dad as too bad a guy, but I know I also have to be honest with them. They can't help if they don't know the real story, and I am seriously itching to hear about their experiences.

When I finish, Hope reaches over and puts her hand on my arm. "I am sorry, dear friend. It must be difficult to be at odds with your father."

I sigh. "That's the weird part. We're at odds, but right now, it's mostly about where I go and what I do. He doesn't know what I know about him, but he's suspicious. He also has this idea that I'm in danger, and I'm not sure why."

"Maybe something to do with his business?" Phonepasit says. "If he is up to no good, he is bound to find no good."

Angoori nods. "Sadly, this is true."

"It will be okay, Coral. We are with you."

I look at my friends and realize I was right—this was exactly what I needed. Feeling better, I help myself to a handful of chocolate-covered raisins. I glance out across the grass, making sure Peeve isn't up to anything he shouldn't be, and a flash of royal blue on the walkway catches my eye. A tree blocks most of my view, but my heart starts to gallop just the same.

Chill out, I tell myself. Thousands of people could be wearing that color today. I grab my water bottle and take a big drink, hoping to calm my nerves.

"Is everything okay, Coral?" Hope's dark eyes scan my face.

"Yes, definitely," I say, deciding that this isn't something I need to worry them with. Not yet. "How about a water toast?" I hold up my bottle. "Here's to all the kids in East Harlem staying healthy. We actually made a difference, my friends."

Phonepasit smiles and lifts her bottle, and Hope does the same. Angoori watches, looking uncertain, but then she joins in with a grin. "Cheers," we all say and take a big drink of this precious stuff we've all promised to protect.

With the thought of our promise, Miriam's face flashes in my mind. "I know we've had some success," I add, "but Miriam was very quick to remind me that we have so much more to do. This is a really big planet."

"I hope we will be together again soon." Phonepasit's eyes look a little sad.

Angoori turns to her. "Look where we are, friend. Look at the four of us, sitting in the park in New York City. Did you ever, in your whole life, think such magic could be possible? Or that it would find you?"

Light fills Phonepasit's face. "You are absolutely right. Thank you, Angoori."

"So, we continue, yes?" I look at each of them, hoping that the training is also unraveling each of their stories. For sure, they can feel how much I care about them, and how happy I am that we get to do this work together.

"And we won't stop, not until we've healed this world."

"No, Coral. We will not stop." Hope takes my hand, and then reaches next to her for Phonepasit's. We all do the same, until the circle is complete and the promise pulses between us.

"Thank you for trusting me, my dear friends." For a moment, I think about how horrible it would have been if even one of them had run away screaming or refused to hear me out. I guess the compass really knew what it was doing.

"We must be the ones to thank you, Coral." Phonepasit gives my hand a squeeze. "My new knowledge and understanding of communicating through the airwaves with airborne insects and birds, are already improving things in Laos. You are the Pathfinder; you lead the way."

I get that helium balloon feeling in my heart again, the one that makes me feel like I can do anything. I look over at Peeve, who's sleeping a few feet away. If only I could have my mom,

Miriam, and Jasper here, my life would be perfect. And maybe someday, after we've shown him a better way, my Dad too.

Peeve seems to feel me looking at him and he sits up, eyes instantly alert.

"Hey, boy," I say. "Want to join the circle?"

It's like he doesn't hear me, which is weird. He just keeps staring over my shoulder. I look back, but I don't see anything.

"You okay, buddy?" I get up from the circle and squat down next to him.

He licks my hand, then looks out across the lawn again. A low growl, almost too low to hear, echoes in his chest. I swallow hard, afraid to follow his gaze. He never growls.

After three deep breaths, I glance over my shoulder again, just in time to see someone slip behind the trees along the walkway. I watch the feet move, lime green sneakers doing a quick power walk. For one quick second, there's a break between branches, and what I see makes me go cold from head to toe.

Blonde hair.

Royal blue nylon.

The compass in my pocket turns icy hot – there's no other way to describe it, like a searing – and starts vibrating so fast, faster than ever before, and suddenly I am vibrating too – I hear Phonepasit's voice ring out, alarmed: "Coral! Coral!!"- a rainbow halo erupts out of the compass, expanding 10 feet above us, then shrinks to encompass all of us, and a FLASH! of light appears so bright it blinds me.

BOOM. Everything goes darkest blue.

About the Author

As a child in suburban Connecticut, intrigued by hidden waterways and secrets buried in the soil, Donna Goodman dreamed of continuing her exploration of nature in faraway places and sharing the magic of water with everyone, everywhere. Decades later, she began work as an educator at the United Nations in New York, teaching peace through science, using magnets and rainbow glasses to help people see the unseen in their own worlds.

In 2002, her dream came true when the UN asked her to write a book about water around the world, _Every Body Counts and Every Drop Matters_. Soon after, she received a call from UNICEF, asking her to develop an online interactive online game called _Water Alert!_ for kids. Since that time, Donna has been a champion of the rights and participation of child and young people in the environment sector for more than 25 years. She was a Program Advisor for UNICEF in Water, Environment and Sanitation as well as Climate Change for 10 years and is the Founder of Earth Child Institute (ECI), an international NGO working with young leaders in more than sixty countries. ECI serves with Special Consultative Status to the United Nations Economic and Social Committee and UN Framework Convention on Climate Change.

In the private sector, Ms Goodman's work has been published by McGraw-Hill, Turner Broadcasting for Cartoon Network and MTV through production of a documentary special program entitled 'Water for Life' featuring Jay-Z. Eager to reach more girls in more countries,

Donna accepted a position as Global Program Director of Swarovski Waterschool, Swarovski's cornerstone community development program bringing water education and stewardship to schools on the major great rivers of the world, including the Amazon; Danube; Ganges; Yangtze; Mekong; Nile; and Mississippi. Finally serving as Executive Producer for a documentary film, entitled <u>Waterschool</u>, now available on Netflix,

Feeling an urgency fueled by our rapidly changing world, Donna sought to reach more kids in the most fun and stimulating ways. This was the spark of the idea for a series of action-adventure middle-grade novels intended to inspire young readers to awaken their unique talents, within a global thrill of magic and miracles hidden in every form of life on Earth. Noting that most popular magical, action/adventure series are led by boys, Donna was inspired to create young female leaders From US to Malawi to Laos to India and to Brazil… all in book one, to forge a path of curiosity, courage to care and skills to take action!

Donna first introduced ECOMASTERS to the world, in a blog post through her role as 'Moderator' for the <u>North American Association of Environmental Educators,</u> K-12 group; and as Keynote speaker to the 2019 International Conference for Education for Sustainability in Delhi, India. Most recently, 5 June 2020, World Environment Day, she unveiled her plan for re-imagining global education in a post COVID-19 world as part of a global webinar organized by the Mobius Foundation.

About the Illustrator

Luisa started her artistic career as a child, experimenting with all sorts of arts and crafts. Since then, she has always been attracted to colors, shapes, materials, fashion, music, food and any type of creative form.

She achieved her bachelor's degree in Milan at IED - Istituto Europeo di Design, with a degree in Illustration and Animation and moved to New York in 2015, to specialize in Graphic Design at Parsons - The New School of Design.

For the past three years she has been working as an art director for an american advertising agency, travelling back and forth between Milan and New York.